Joan Marysmith lives in Leicester with her husband; her three children are grown up and live in or around London. A growing number of grandchildren are a source of pleasure and time consumption. When she's not with them or writing, her favourite occupation is travelling. Her first novel, *Holy Aspic*, is also published by Black Swan.

Also by Joan Marysmith

HOLY ASPIC

and published by Black Swan

WATERWINGS

Joan Marysmith

WATERWINGS

A BLACK SWAN BOOK : 0 552 99689 0

First publication in Great Britain

PRINTING HISTORY
Black Swan edition published 1997

All of the characters in this book are fictitious, and any resemblance to actual persons, living or dead, is purely coincidental.

Set in 11/13½pt Linotype Melior by County Typesetters, Margate, Kent

Black Swan Books are published by Transworld Publishers Ltd, 61–63 Uxbridge Road, London W5 5SA, in Australia by Transworld Publishers (Australia) Pty Ltd, 15–25 Helles Avenue, Moorebank, NSW 2170 and in New Zealand by Transworld Publishers (NZ) Ltd, 3 William Pickering Drive, Albany, Auckland.

Reproduced, printed and bound in Great Britain by Cox & Wyman Ltd, Reading, Berks.

Dedication

For my daughters Caroline and Rachel who,
though nothing like Perdita, are proof that
even teenagers can become lovely human beings.

Acknowledgements

Although I have not quoted directly from any of the following works, I acknowledge that all I know of the Celtic tradition comes from them – and not only what features in this novel, but much more of interest and enjoyment besides.

Pagan Celtic Britain, Anne Ross, Constable 1993 edition;
The Celtic Year, Shirley Toulson, Element 1994 reprint;
The Celtic Shaman, John Matthews, Element 1995 reprint;
Mysterious Britain, Janet & Colin Bord, Thorsons 1995 edition;
The Elements of Celtic Christianity, Anthony Duncan, Element 1993 reprint;
The Elements of the Celtic Tradition, Caitlin Matthews, Element 1994 reprint;
Celtic Lore and Druidic Ritual, Rhiannon Ryall, Capall Bann Publishing 1994;
Sacred Times, William Bloom, Findhorn Press 1990;
Our Pagan Christmas, R.J. Condon, National Secular Society 1974.

Death of Summer

'Tiberius was deprived of his manhood last week, remember, Brigid.' Jan Morrow stuffed a gadget for heating water into her handbag, as if expecting a crisis even before Heathrow. 'Fishy treats to console. In the pantry. Bottom shelf.'

Brigid *was* a woman of compassion, but not reckless with it. Feeding fishy treats to a recently neutered cat wasn't her idea of a good time. Fastidious and aloof, she watched Jan cram electric flex into her handbag, nothing like all set for her world trip. Jan grabbed a half used tube of sun cream from the table. Its sell-by date was two years previous.

'Pantry. Bottom shelf,' repeated Brigid. Now the Morrows were on the point of leaving she wanted to shoo them out like their animals, she wanted them gone. She needed to start repairing her life. That was why she was here.

'Tassie, the tortoiseshell with bad breath. Don't let her bring in mice. She mislays them. Been known to create a plague.' Jan Morrow laughed artificially. She'd told that joke before. She showed her large yellow teeth, sensitive as a gelding's, and her eyes compressed to cotton threats behind emerald framed specs.

Jan and Philip Morrow stood in front of their large Victorian home. The ochre and dirty pink of the stone softened the nineteenth-century solemnity. Heedlessly transferred carrycots and wayward golf bags had gouged blue paint off the doorframe and left black, neglected scars. Jan searched for last minute instructions, her chubby face slanted to the sky and eyes shut tight in concentration. Brigid thought she resembled a hibernating wombat emerging.

Two small suitcases didn't seem enough for a three month trip though there was a rucksack for when they went *indigenous*, as Philip put it. 'It's frightfully interesting to know about the natives,' he said. Brigid thought the rucksack would be the only indication of when they *were* indigenous, as Jan looked exactly the same whether she were here in Northumbria or in London. She was always in brown. Today she wore a nutmeg crimplene dress, jazzed up with an adjustable webbing belt. She didn't favour natural fibres. Her tights were the colour of bitter tea, and her sensible buckle sandals had thick, tan composite soles. Her fawn hair was scraped into a mean bun on top of her head, half an inch off centre.

'I've bought shorts, you know,' she said, as if reading Brigid's thoughts. 'Khaki.' She shook her head in wonder. 'I know I'm eccentric, dear, but think of all the great women explorers. Where would the world be without its characters?' She chortled and a spat of saliva landed on her chin.

Brigid smiled automatically. Jan Morrow was as eccentric as a house sparrow. Eccentricity inspires affection, banality doesn't. 'Shorts sound fine,' she said.

'Oh, do you think so?' There was a note of resentment. 'They're quite long shorts.'

'She'll put the fear of God into the natives in those all right. She's what the Empire was made of,' said Philip.

His own synthetic trousers had a tired shine round the buttocks.

It wasn't money that had deserted the Morrows, but style. They owned the impressive nineteenth-century house, and the furniture to go with it, all inherited from Philip's father, but they weren't in tune. They matched neither the Victorian Chippendale furniture in their dining-room nor the black highly decorated range in the kitchen. Some curtains had no linings and Philip watched wrestling on television. They grew no herbs but bedded out the flower bed under the dining-room window with red, white and blue half hardy annuals.

'I'm taking with me,' said Philip, 'a copy of the poems of William Wordsworth, and several postcards of the painting of Wellington at Waterloo. Any truck from the French, and I'll stick one over their bidet.' He snorted, remarkably pig like. First-hand knowledge of French washing habits substitutes for an understanding of their culture. Jan nodded approval. Nationalism was essential when travelling.

Brigid had arrived in time for a lunch of fatty lamb stew, christened by Jan as the bran tub pottage, and an opportunity to make use of leftovers. Lumps of swede nestled alongside globules of cheddar cheese, under a crust of crumbled Ryvita biscuits. An occasional hard-boiled egg bobbed jauntily to the surface. Tinned pears spread with marmalade followed.

'What will you do with your time?' Jan asked, scraping round the jar.

'When Rupert died I gave up an interior design course. I might get some books from the library. I'd like to finish it eventually.'

Jan's small eyes gleamed behind her spectacles. 'Feel

free to experiment here,' she said, 'painting a room or anything like that.' Free offers were the mainstay of Jan's domestic economics. 'The garden always looks a bit of a mess,' she added.

Brigid watched marmalade sliding uncaringly off the wet surface of the pear and wondered how she'd allowed herself to be drawn into this situation. Why was she to be a house sitter for this ghastly couple for the next three months? It had been all *too* easy.

Philip Morrow, despite the apparent lack of intelligence, was a successful businessman. He wasn't dependent on inherited income. He manufactured fake ethnic jewellery and bowls and sometimes fabrics, which he supplied to street markets, craft fairs and shops where those with a taste for foreign culture liked to browse. There were none of the shipping costs of the real thing. Furthermore, an absence of any reference to Taiwan or South Korea seemed sufficient proof of their authenticity.

Philip stayed two days a week in London supervising these projects, and sleeping in the London flat, which was in the same area of Wimbledon as Brigid's home. He spent the rest of his time in the North. Jan sometimes came to London with him. Brigid had met the Morrows in July at a dinner party given by Esther and Harvey who were avid meal providers. Their two favourite forms of entertaining were Hungarian nights and Kashmiri evenings. The difference between the two was whether Esther put paprika or cumin into the mince. Without Rupert, Brigid became an oddity as a guest, a bit of a problem being on her own, and so often got lumped together with other problems. The Morrows' sense of style was a serious problem to Esther, but she felt obliged to have them round as

Harvey bought Bengali-style rice bowls from Philip for when they gave *really* big Kashmiri evenings. No-one ever used the Morrows as guests to impress their other friends. As a problem, they were invited round the same evening as Brigid. It was a K evening.

She was surprised when over the dahl and coconut-flavoured rice Jan suggested she might like a break in the country, to get over Rupert's death. 'Why not a few months away from it all? You could have our house in Northumbria while we go on our world adventure.' Only later did it transpire there were cats to tend, and Brigid would be doing Jan a favour as a burglar deterrent.

The cats were characters and would cause endless anxiety in a cattery. Only later, when Harvey explained to the Morrows that Brigid had temporary financial difficulties, did Jan offer to pay for the feline nurturing. Rupert hadn't expected to die, his will was vague, and his money inconveniently tied up. The solicitors were taking an age to sort it out.

There'd been a detached unreality about the way the plan progressed, a slow-moving inevitability, like walking under water. It eventually led to this foul lunch, and now, to standing in the drive of Highmoor House while Jan and Philip dithered about moving off.

Jan fed herself inelegantly into the car, and said over her shoulder as she strapped up, 'The kids *might* turn up. It's unlikely. They're so busy. Such successful lives. Though there's always Simon. God knows where he is.' She put her head out of the window again, this time her face lighting up. 'There's Tara, remember, the Russian blue. Unbelievably fastidious. Milk out of the bottle, not a carton. Full cream.'

The customized mango Jaguar with Philip's initials

incorporated into the number plate finally disappeared out of the drive. Brigid could hear it ploughing down the road to the village, then in the silence, imagined it weaving through the trees towards the main road. The recollection of Jan, so confident with so little justification, leaping into the car and into her adventure, diminished. The place felt more tranquil for her going.

Brigid felt a momentary panic, like being knocked sideways by a wave. Initially it seemed a godsend to get away from the well-meaning sympathy, and the unspoken pity. Her friends, Murray and Jennifer, took her to see *Les Misérables* and spent the evening apologizing for not choosing something more cheerful, though it *was* good, wasn't it? Friends had been there for her, had been kind to her. Murray and Jennifer defined her lifestyle. The four of them always had barbecues in the summer with steaks and sangria. They played tennis in the light evenings and bridge when the evenings were dark. They went to concerts and Italian restaurants. Now, neither spoke of Rupert, nor of anything to do with him. She felt threatened by their silence. It reinforced the pain.

Here, at last, she was free of sympathy, but her new solitude became a threat of another nature. Loneliness. Ahead of her stretched three months of facing her loss, nights of black emptiness, days of never being able to understand why. This was the wrong time of the year to make a fresh start anywhere, it was a bleak interval, a time of sorrow and darkness.

Brigid made tea with a teabag in a mug, and sat in the last of the autumn sun, wondering how to begin this new life. She normally had a cup of Rose Pouchong with a teapot on a tray ready for a second.

She sat now at a stranger's front door with a mug on the step beside her, too despondent to find a garden chair, or a sheltered spot on the grass at the back. She was alone in this large, strange house but for the cats. It was a mistake.

She crossed her legs, and stretched her spine, sitting tall, an elegant woman in a cream silk shirt, and a neutral cashmere sweater thrown over her shoulders. She had perfect nails, though she never wore varnish. Anyone looking at her, could be certain her toenails were equally immaculate. Her long slim feet in ankle boots were neat extensions of her sage-coloured ski pants. She was distinguished by her hair, cut as only Rolando could do it. He was a genius, and her hair his creation. It transformed her otherwise ordinary face. The hair was ruffled now by the Northumbrian wind. Nothing soothing about that. Its freedom and sense of renewal were alien. Not an experience Brigid needed.

She warmed her hands round the blue-striped mug, and grimaced at the bitterness of the tea. She'd left the bag in too long. She leaned against the door frame, shaded by the portico, that classical pretension of the Victorian high-flying builder. Behind her was the shade of the deep square hall and an empty stillness. If she went into the house she'd have to move, be a person. Here on the step, she remained in limbo, hovering. She hadn't sat on a front step since she was a child. So slovenly.

She was still like a cat, as the late sun moved across the oval patch of grass in front of the house, with its gravel path all around for the carriages to sweep through. Between the beech trees marking the front boundary she could see the valley beyond with its cultivated fields and patches of woodland, late crops and trimmed hedges. Beyond the valley lay the Cheviot hills, serene and aloof. She watched each bird as it dived from tree to bush, from bush to earth, and felt totally apart from the order of the land around her. Hers was an order of the vermouth before dinner, the dill in the sauce, the Body Shop face scrub, not the call of the earth. Beyond the cultivated land lay the A1 as it carried the traffic between Newcastle and Berwick-upon-Tweed, her last link with civilization. Further out was the sea, the ever cold, loveless North Sea, with its mighty waves, and its hints of ice and death. She was separated from this place as if by something as tangible and as specific as water.

What was there here for her? Was it peopled with oddities like Jan and Philip? The only person she'd seen as she drove from the village was a man walking a Shetland sheepdog. He was tall and thin, in a waxed jacket obviously made well before they became fashionable. He started as the car passed him, and stooped down to stare into the window. She could still see his large pale hazel eyes with their look of disbelief as he looked at her. It seemed obvious even then she wasn't at one with this place.

'I'm an island,' she said aloud to the garden, 'and I'm totally isolated.' She felt lonelier than she'd ever felt before.

This might be the final sun of the year since it was the last day of October. If she stayed very still, and focused on the alien landscape, feeding on its strangeness, her mind might shut out what happened in February.

As she overlooked these unfriendly hills Rupert seemed to join her. His look rebuked her for sitting on the step, his distaste for the orange rim of tea sediment inside the mug showed in the quiver of his upper lip.

'Comfort me,' she whispered. 'If you want to haunt me, at least come as a friend.'

When she saw him in her mind he was always at a distance, not as he'd been in life, close and loving, and always approving. She never tired of looking at him, admiring that over-long nose, his opaque brown eyes, the cream grey of his skin, his hair cut short to his well-shaped head. He'd been designed as a whole, everything about him was right. Spring and all the summer had passed since he'd died, and there'd always been this distance between them. It was because . . . but she couldn't bring herself to think about it. Please take away . . . that memory.

Who exactly *was* Brigid she wondered, if not defined by the order of her life with Rupert, the meals and activities with her friends, her hair cut by Rolando?

Below, in the valley, a van lurched along the road from Hepburn to The Charltons. Idly, she wondered if it would go north up the A1 to Berwick-upon-Tweed, or south to Alnwick. It might even go across to the coast, to the clean sweeping sands where the breezes always blew. It was too far away for Brigid to hear the engine. She watched it with the lethargy of one not totally conscious of the world around her. The van was painted a subtle lemon, not a commercial colour. In a moment it would disappear beyond the hill and she would never know whether it went to Seahouses, or to the north. She was wrong. It paused, and wobbled its way round the corner, turning right into the lane that lead up to Highmoor House.

Brigid picked up the mug still half full of cold tea, and slipped inside the house. She closed the front door and went up to the turn in the stairs where a window overlooked the front drive. Above her, the fustiness of the large landing with all its doors firmly shut was like a blanket. When the van went, she would throw open all the heavy doors and pull up every sash window. She would clear away the smell of the Morrows, and blow through her own soul at the same time. She licked her finger and wiped it under her eyes, making sure there was no smudged mascara.

Who'd arrive in a van? Surely none of the Morrow children. The elder son had a Range Rover and dogs, the daughter had children in designer clothes. She'd met them in London staying with their parents, when she'd been completing arrangements. The son and daughter weren't like their mother. The money and house had made *them* fashionable. They'd never arrive in a van, especially not one she could now see was decorated with a meandering turquoise pattern. There was another son, whom she'd not met. He wasn't spoken about. It seemed likely this was a gang coming to clean out the furniture.

The van struggled with the hill. Brigid could hear angry revving, and then the scrunch of the gravel as it cornered badly into the drive. She must show the house was occupied by opening the landing window, and, if necessary, pretend to shout back to someone within. She waited until she could see exactly who these people were.

The driver jumped down, a youth with a mass of auburn curly hair. Even from the window she could see his very large eyes matched his hair colour exactly. He leaned back against the bonnet of the van, his arms crossed, scanning the house. It wasn't the intense stare of a prospective burglar, it was a lazy look, uncaring, as if he just happened to be in this place, the idlest of curiosities. Brigid guessed he was either particularly intelligent, to match the intensity of his eyes, or exceptionally stupid, with his blank, uncaring stare. One or the other, nothing between.

Someone else opened the back door of the van a few inches, cautiously, in contrast to the driver. Someone *was* surveying the house this time. Brigid stood back slightly, so she couldn't be seen. The door opened further, and a head emerged. The head was hairless and male. It didn't have the blue tinge of a shaven head, where follicles are harbouring blunted filaments. Instead there was a waxy shine. The face had strong classy bones, and a full sensuous mouth. The surprise were the eyes, very dark, like two shining coffee beans, and they had dark thick lashes, in startling contrast to the polished skull.

He inspected every window. Brigid leaned back further into the shadow. Only then did he climb out of the van, emerging slowly, because of his caftan. It was a pale sap green, and swirled round his legs like whisked guacamole. Momentarily, Brigid wondered if a mutant Hari Krishna had arrived.

He was no more than a youth and small, only about five foot two. He stood with his legs astride and held his hands palms upwards, looking as if he'd conjured the house out of the air. Brigid decided despite the potentially menacing skinhead image, nothing else about him seemed burglar material. A caftan would hopelessly hamper a quick getaway.

She opened the sash, and leaned out. 'You are?'

The youth stared, wary again. His hands dropped down to his sides.

'Yes?' Brigid made it clear she was in charge. 'You are?'

Perhaps because she wasn't Jan Morrow, the youth relaxed.

'A lady is revealed. Hi.' He smiled now, and the darkness of the eyes in contrast to the pale skull gave him an unnerving intensity. 'I need to know your name.'

The other youth was raising his eyebrows up and down, as if the sight of Brigid disorientated him.

'Brigid.'

'Of course. The house sitter. Supplier of comestibles to the felines. These things come to be known. I'm the prodigal. The nutter. The one the neighbours wink at each other about. I am Si.' He held out his arms, welcoming Brigid to his world.

Samhain

The Celtic year was dominated by solstices and equinoxes, by the turning of the seasons. Theirs was a pastoral society, totally dependent on the sun and rain, so it was not surprising their gods and goddesses lived within the realms of nature.

The Celtic year began at Samhain, which was the start of November. Since the Celtic day began in the evening at sundown, Samhain included the last night of October, which Christians call 'The eve of all Saints' and the less religious know as Hallowe'en. While today we see the year beginning with spring which is young, and progressing through to winter, the pagan Celts began their year with the coming of the dark, and progressing through to the light of summer and the fruition of autumn. It was a vision of enhanced optimism, and more truthful to the earth.

The term Samhain meant the death of summer, and in one way the winter months were a dead time, a time of sorrow and darkness. Yet it was also a fallow time, a period of rest and rejuvenation, and a time of reflection and planning, a time to ponder the future. Because the grain was sown in the early winter, new life was already in the earth. Beneath the soil the seeds held the germ of what was to come, they contained the essence of spring. The surface of the world may have been bleak, but beneath in the soul of the earth, in the heart of Gaia, it was a time of hope.

At the very start of Samhain, when dark fell on the last

day of what the Romans later named October, the Celts saw the world to be at its most transparent. The distinction between the material and eternal worlds scarcely existed, and it was easier then than at any other time to communicate with ancestors.

Such Celtic beliefs flourish today, under the guises of faiths that have taken them over. The Romans coming later attached their fruit festival to Samhain, which they held in honour of Pomona. We see the use of pumpkins at Hallowe'en, and occasionally the game of bobbing for apples. The Samhain bonfire was replaced by that for Guy Fawkes, and Christians still celebrate All Souls' Day on November 2.

The Celtic Way, A.B.W.

'Jan mentioned some family. She was rather vague,' Brigid admitted.

'Would be. Always hopes I'm not really here. OK, so I'm Si, and this is Dessi. Short for Desmond and also for disciple.' He jerked his head towards the auburn-haired youth still lounging on the bonnet of the van.

'Is it just you? Or is the rest of the family coming?'

'*They* come when the onspring *are* home, I come when they're not. Could you let us in? Do you need identification? There's my birthmark.'

'That won't be necessary.'

'No trouble, darlin'. It's on my elbow.'

Brigid glanced in the hall mirror on the way to the door. She tweaked up the collar of her shirt. Two of the three cats glided into her path. It was feeding time. She shoved them aside with her foot and opened the outsize front door.

Si strode in, right hand raised, palm forward as if driving a way through the air before him. 'You can feel them, can't you? The negative vibrations.' He shifted

Brigid out of the way by her shoulders. He was smaller than she was, but she obediently moved over. She hovered by the sitting-room door, while he paced into each corner of the hall, holding his palms up, eyes closed and face directed to the ceiling like an optimistic green cricket. 'Feel the new resonance.' Dessi watched him, yawning and leaning on the door post. Si fluttered his fingers to indicate showering. 'Prana,' he said.

'Sanskrit,' said Dessi, 'for invisible energy.' Intelligence momentarily filtered through like a reluctant sun between leaden clouds.

Si whirled round on his heels to face her. 'Better?' He smiled at Brigid, a lazy, enveloping smile, challenging her to disagree.

'Much better,' said Dessi, who saw it was now safe to follow Si inside. Brigid noticed he moved close to the walls as if he weren't happy in open space.

'I'll clean where we'll eat.' Si wafted into the inner hall, and through to the kitchen. He found serious energy blockages. He lingered over the sink and Brigid wondered if he'd have an influence on the drains. Jan was a woman not closely acquainted with a bottle of Jeyes. He worked his way across the orange painted cupboards, and among the bentwood chairs, the sort found in schools when Brigid was young. He hovered over the cooker, which currently failed to radiate any sort of warm glow, even though Jan assured her there had been an oil delivery last week.

He contemplated the kitchen table. 'Formica,' he said. 'Not receptive.'

In the fading afternoon light, Si's sap green robe glowed vibrantly as winter jasmine gleams in the dusk. He was radiant among the tasteless clutter of Jan's kitchen, a butterfly on a heap of cinders. 'What's on for supper? I'm a vegetarian.'

'I'll look in the pantry. I don't think there's much.'

'The world is a wonderful place. It will provide. Don't bother about trivialities.'

Dessi nodded. He transferred himself from the door post to the range, warming his back against its non-existant comfort.

'Next. Purification.' Si looked down at the dirt on his feet, grey and ingrained around the straps of his sandals. He waved his hands hopefully over them, but to no avail. 'A soap job.'

Dessi said, 'He never fancies a shower in the mornings.'

'A bath. What a good idea,' said Brigid, looking at Si's feet as well, 'though I've no idea what the water's like.' She washed her own hands under the tap, and rinsed out the tea mug. She scoured away the orange rim of tannin stain.

He looked out of the window. 'Two worlds coming together,' he mused. 'The darkness will overcome the light. We sense what we cannot see. It will be temporary.' He turned round and looked triumphantly at Brigid.

'I think we all know day follows night,' she said.

Si, unsquashed, went upstairs to purify the upper landing, before taking a bath. Brigid appraised the pantry shelves. They revealed more of the Morrows' lifestyle in a profusion of peanut butter and honey jars, the contents all in progressive stages of crystallization, alongside tins of salmon and luncheon meat. There was an entire shelf given over to tins of cat food, all animal gourmet and speciality brands. There was a winter's supply of cornflakes and tinned raspberries, but a dearth of anything useful like wholemeal flour, olive oil, or black peppercorns.

There was a solitary banana gone well over in a glass fruit bowl on the table. She would throw it away later when she located the waste bin. The fridge, a monster with a curved top, throbbing in the corner, held frozen peas, an out-of-date and encrusted bottle of Marie-Rose salad dressing, and four soggy tomatoes. There was, however, a carton on the draining board holding fresh bread and cheese, both unfortunately ready sliced and perspiring, a bottle of full cream milk and six eggs. If Jan thought this was a starter pack for a holiday apartment, she'd forgotten the fresh fruit and local wine.

Dessi brought in some gear from the van, crumpled clothes, trainers caked in mud and a laundry bag. Once he got moving, he moved fast, his chestnut hair bouncing round his face purposefully. It was in decision making he slowed up. Back downstairs he stood indecisively by the kitchen door.

Tiberius, a grossly overweight and now neutered tom-cat strode as imperiously as his namesake into the kitchen and stood squarely in front of Brigid. He bellowed, face distorted into a snarl. Tara and Tassie lined up behind him. A congregation of dishes and milk bowls clustered glutinously together under the table. The cats were hungry now, rubbing round her legs, getting under her feet. Brigid shuddered when Tiberius wove himself round her ankle affectionately in marked contrast to his grimace.

'That lot outside the back door,' said Brigid pointing to the feline crockery.

'I'll feed them,' said Dessi and spent five minutes in the pantry deciding which variety to open despite the mewing and yelling at him to get on with it.

Brigid, tired of waiting for the sound of bath water gushing away, grilled the tomatoes. They were too far gone for a salad. She decided on omelettes, and tried to grate the plastic cheese slices, but they broke into rubbery gobs. 'Get on with it,' she called to Dessi. The noise of the cats was making her touchy.

She threw the eggs into the pan. What did it matter if they got overcooked and leathery because Si dawdled in the bath? She'd sacrificed the comforts of Wimbledon to give her soul room, she'd braved the loneliness of Northumbria to find space, and on the very first night, she was saddled with a New Age mystic soaking overlong in the bath, and another dithering inadequately in the pantry.

'If you *do* manage to feed the cats, would you then lay the table, please.' She sounded more sarcastic than she meant. She suddenly noticed that the range was warming up, humming like a cat purring.

Dessi emerged from the pantry with a Tuna Tempter in one hand and a Pheasant Feast in the other. 'Got down to two,' he said. 'What do you think?' His auburn eyes were wide and round.

Brigid wished she hadn't sounded so cross. 'Go for it,' she said, wielding the spatula to let the raw egg run under the cooked. The butter was turning too dark a brown, well beyond the nutty stage. The soft floppiness of the eggs had reached optimum density and was about to become elastic. The toast sizzled on the hotplate poised on the point of burning.

Si sauntered into the kitchen wearing jeans and a white muslin shirt tied at the waist. His chest, thrust out like a pouter pigeon, was a ribscape of dark curly hair. 'Bet the onspring locked the cellar and kept the key. Being perceptive, I got a copy last visit.'

He unlocked the cellar which led off the inner hall, and clattered down the stone steps, returning with a Pouilly-Fumé, and a Vosne-Romanée.

'Who'd believe a man'd drink this with the *hausfrau*'s cooking? One of life's insoluble mysteries. She once did scrambled eggs in a particularly creative mood. Came out like tennis balls. Literally bounced. The old man will down a Gevrey-Chambertin with cornflakes and raspberry jam. Buys on price.'

Si pulled the corks, put the bottles on the table, and drew up a chair, scraping it noisily along the floor. He poured the wine carelessly into glasses, downed his own, and filled it again. Without waiting for the others he sucked up omelette like an industrial hoover. 'This wouldn't bounce,' he said, his mouth full. 'Honestly. It's good to be civilized again.'

Brigid stood it as a compliment and tried not to wince as he rammed home some toast. It was the result of his nomadic lifestyle with the van. Dessi cut his omelette into ten segments and his fork gyrated over the plate until he decided which to impale.

Brigid ate slowly herself, wielding her fork with the grace of one who only toys with food. Eating with just a fork is slow and helps one to stay slim. 'Are you on your way somewhere?' She spoke lightly. Sharing meals with Si wasn't going to bring calm.

He crunched into the last piece of toast, spraying burned particles over the table. 'This is my home. It's where I lay my head. Why should I move on?' He peeled the gone over banana and offered half to Brigid. She took it, mesmerized. The brown pulp melted on her tongue, fermented and alcholic, as if Si had changed banana into grapes.

Brigid said, 'It's not my home. I'll go.'

'I don't like cats. I'd forget to buy the tins. They'd get feral. Nothing worse than an uncultivated cat.'

'So you're staying some time?'

'We may stay,' mused Si. 'Or we may not. What do you think, Dessi?'

'Might do.'

'Anyway, *you* can't go Brigid. You've got to feed me. Dessi's a long way off being cordon bleu.'

'What?' Brigid finished the last of her omelette, leaving the cheese which would have made a merry bouncing companion to Jan's scrambled egg. 'I'm staying on as a cook?'

Si smiled across the table at her. It was a fantastic smile, and he knew it. His face became all innocent eyes and warmth. The glow more than compensated for his eating habits. He kept on smiling, saying nothing, making the world seem more fun. He never worked on his charm, not since he discovered he had it, anyway.

'We'll see how we manage,' Brigid said against her better judgement, having difficulty not smiling back.

He nodded. With his elbows on the table, he cradled his skull in his hands, and sat massaging his bald head with his fingers. He stared ahead at another horizon. Brigid averted her gaze.

'It's his head,' said Dessi.

'I can see that.'

'The others won't be coming for a while.' Si kept on with his fingers.

'What others?' She hoped she still sounded calm.

'Followers. People. Friends. That sort of thing. I fancy a commune.'

* * *

Si was speculative. It was ten-thirty. 'You *could* begin with what happened,' he said, 'but it's better to begin with *when*. Time is more cosmic than place.'

'Sorry?'

'You have a problem, Brigid.'

'No I don't.'

'Brigid, I'm called where I'm needed.' His eyes were so deep-set and dark, yet they carried a hint of green. Brigid was reminded of seaweed in dark rocky pools, set in white rock.

'It's impossible to ignore the energy,' he explained. 'There isn't good and evil. There's only energy. Positive or negative. Negative energy is draining. You're giving out negative energy and it's making me tired.'

'I *am* tired.'

'Brigid. We're trying to find the *when*.' Si held his hands out in front of him, about a foot apart, and moved them about a little, like a rugby player handling the ball. 'I'd put it at about six months ago. Not less. You're not in acute shock. Not much more, perhaps seven months. Your spirit's still crying out in pain.' He nodded slowly. 'Yes. I think we've found the when. I'm right, aren't I? When was when?'

'Eight months ago, the funeral. Rupert and I were very happy. I'm sorry, Si. I don't want to talk.'

'Fine. We'll exit right here. When you want to come back to it, know I've got it tabbed. There'll be less to explain. I see it was more than the death. You said funeral. What made you say *funeral*? Why not eight months ago, he *died*? Something made the funeral worse than the death. I'm right, aren't I? Yes? Know you can come in at that point. Feel you can share it with me.'

'*Thank* you, Si.' Brigid aped his psycho speak, then

got off the subject. 'You're here because your parents are away.'

'Yeah. Highmoor House is better than the van. Highmoor House *sans* the onspring must be better than the van. Actually, there's nothing much wrong with the van itself. It's where to put the damn thing and the people in the other vans. They're not like us.'

'I see. Van snobbery.' Brigid was still annoyed.

'OK, there are serious spiritual people out there. I mean *really* serious people. Off the floor with it. Fan*tas*tic. But there's all the hangers-on. Yuppies slumming it at the weekend. Terribly green, my dear, but only part-time. You've got the great unwashed hoards living in vans to avoid obligations imposed by the state. However, they're not deterred from obtaining the benefits thereof. They ignore the niceties of the sewerage system. Think anything biodegradable can be dumped behind a fence. There are those who've traded in big God because he's not much help, and are giving the pagan gods a go. Sometimes you *have* to get away.' He leaned his head on his hands once more, and probed the shining skull.

'It's a dilemma. If you want credibility you need a proper job. If you go the whole hog, you look unhinged.' Dessi frowned. 'It's not fair. All religions in the past had a nomadic tradition.'

'What would the middle classes make of Jesus today? Tell him to wash his hands for a start. Get down the Job Centre.' Si had now worked round to his temples.

Dessi nodded, nostalgia overwhelming him. 'The Tories wouldn't like his dodgy work ethic. Where would Jesus be today with Old Labour gone?'

'Negative energy,' said Si, relinquishing his scalp. 'You're being destructive.' He went to the window and stared out. 'All Hallows' eve. The great fire festival. The Peace fire.'

'He's getting back,' Dessi explained. 'To the roots. I'm not talking about his hair.'

Tassie and Tara, asleep in front of the range twitched in their sleep. They lay on a frayed piece of carpet, whose looped fronds were a hazard so near the stove. Tiberius was out in the night trying to recover his lost libido.

'Candles,' said Si. 'No time to get bonfire fuel. Candles will suffice perfectly. In fact, candles are better, more symbolic. More subtle.' He rummaged through the cupboard under the sink and took half a dozen from a large box. Jan always kept a good stock. Highmoor House had unreliable wiring. The Morrows used an economic electrician to deal with problems, and they tended to recur. Si stuck the candles in wine bottles from the waste bin and milk bottles from the draining board. He plugged the wide necks with newspaper, and put all but two on the window sill. He gazed into the flames and the light illuminated the hollows of his skull.

'What about the dishes?' Brigid asked.

Si turned to her, and his face was full of a childlike wonder. 'When we get back darlin'. You're too mundane. The light will guide lost spirits to us. We may commune. Anyway, I'm expecting to discover my totem beast soon.' He let himself out of the back door. Dessi followed him. Through the window, she could see the flickering candles as Si and Dessi patrolled the garden hoping to make contact with a stray soul.

After five minutes she pulled up the sash and called, 'Come in. I want to lock up. The house is still my responsibility.'

Si came to the window. He smiled, sinister in the candlelight. 'Bit short of ancestors out here.'

Brigid looked round the charmless kitchen, and went into the sitting-room to find a drinks cupboard. She discovered some whisky among other bottles on a barbecue trolley behind a sofa, and poured herself a large one. What a lousy day, littered with ghastly and mad Morrows. She went back to the kitchen for some tap water, in the predictable absence of the bottled sort.

Si and Dessi came in.

'That's it then, is it?'

'Too rushed to create the ambience.' Si sat on the back doorstep, eyes closed, letting cold air into the kitchen. 'Wild Herne the hunter, show me my totem beast. I'll travel with you over the mountain and into the wild plain, and there you shall make the creature apparent to me.'

'I bet it won't be a horse,' said Dessi. 'Probably a duck or something.'

'Could you shut the door, please?'

Si ignored them both.

'Nothing doing?' Dessi was sympathetic when five minutes passed without any revelation breaking in on the meditation. Si stood up and shut the back door.

Suddenly, with a blood-curdling screech, Tiberius came through the cat flap like a cannon ball. He leaped onto the kitchen table and stood shaking and hissing, eyes firmly on the cat door. His fur was puffed up to make him pass for a tiger. He growled like a dog.

'That's it, Dessi. The spirits have made contact. This could be my totem beast. The one to guide me.'

Dessi whispered, 'What should we do now?'

'Got to make certain.' Si found the fish-shaped cat

treats in the pantry. They smelled of putrid mackerel. He sat on the floor and held them out in his hand. Tiberius got wind of them and since nothing had followed him in through the cat flap, poured himself off the table. Tassie and Tara woke and ambled over.

Around him sat the three cats. Where Tassie and Tiberius were overweight, Tara grew ever thinner, disdaining all tinned food. She lived only on wildlife which gave her worms, like a model who eats only raw steak. She sat before Si, keeping an eye on the other two, though not the slightest interested in treats.

The brown shapes lay in his open hand and little by little, with the thrill of theft, Tiberius and Tassie stole them away, and hid under the table crunching. Only Tara remained staring at him with her disdainful green eyes.

Si closed his eyes, whispering. 'Show me my guiding spirit. Tiberius, give me a sign. You're a lion of a cat.'

'You know he's been snipped?' Brigid said.

Si opened his eyes. 'That's the onspring for you. Muck up everything.'

Tara remained before him with a knowing gleam in her narrow green eyes. She and Si stared at one another. A Russian blue is never the first to lower her lids in an eyelock. Eventually Si was forced to look down. Tara looked amused. She stood up, stretched luxuriously, and stalked away to the cat flap, with deliberate paws and tail aloft.

'Is it *you*? Are you my totem beast?'

Tara stopped at the back door and turned to stare at him. Her eyes narrowed further, she almost smiled. Then she strode on and poured herself out into the night.

'That's it. That's her. My totem beast. You can see how mystical she is.'

'Does it matter it being a she?' Dessi asked.

Brigid slammed the kitchen door behind her and went to her bedroom. On the way she collected the whisky bottle from the sitting-room.

Brigid woke when the phone rang early. She had a headache, the result of too much whisky last night, and the stress of the whole of yesterday. Six-thirty in the morning is a bad time for phoning. The ringing penetrated the thick bedroom door. It was still going when Brigid got to the hall.

'You took ages to answer,' said Perdita, her voice bubbling and accusing, loving and careless, all at the same time, the welcome voice of Brigid's last born.

'You're up early. Lovely to hear from you.' She could imagine Perdita sleep kissed, in an oversized night-shirt, surrounded by yesterday's clothes on the floor. Admittedly the Brixton flat was short of storage space.

'I've not gone to bed yet. Are you all right in the north?'

'Of course I am. Everything the same in the south?'

'Pretty blissful.'

'I hope you're behaving.'

'Mum. Life is for living. L. I. F. E. I've only got one. No-one's going to curb me.'

'Why don't you come up for the weekend? Bring Mark.'

'It's Jez now.'

'Bring Jez then.'

'I'll see. There's a lot on at the moment. Jez knows where people are. He *is* the scene. It's absolutely wherever he's at. Just wanted to know you're not feeling too awful. Not lonely or anything.'

'A weekend in the country,' said Brigid, trying to make it sound attractive. 'We could have a log fire.'

'Mum. There's so much on. Life is scrummy.'

'The son of the house has turned up.'

'Could have tempted me once. Not with Jez around though. Fwaah. He's all man. Know what I mean? OK, Mum. Great. See you.'

'What about coming up for Christmas?'

'Yeah. Have to see. Could do.'

'Perdita . . .'

'Cheers.' The phone went uncaringly dead.

Brigid washed in cold water, not through choice, dressed, and went to the kitchen, feeling better for hearing Perdita. She went out to where the back porch was a clutter of lacrosse sticks and cricket bats and a broken umbrella. There was a tray of stale cat litter, which seemed superfluous to the feline arrangements, and there were several plastic pots cradling the remains of dead plants, the soil shrivelled away from the sides. She tripped over a surfboard. Angrily, she kicked it out of the way.

The year had changed. Yesterday there was warmth in the sun. Now there was a chilly mist that held the promise of winter frost. There was a small, untidy terrace made of local hewn stone, uneven and dark grey. Beyond, the grass was once a tennis lawn, now humpy and weed strewn, flanked by borders of shrubs and flowers chosen for their durability. The perennials hadn't been cut down for the winter and were yellowing, unhealthy clumps. There was a small vegetable patch at the end of the grass, and then came the rough fells crawling out to the Cheviot hills in the distance.

The garden was disorderly, like her life. The hills beyond were free, which she wasn't. Brigid could imagine how the borders could look if they were not two rigidly straight lines, if they were in sympathy with the country beyond. It all needed getting into shape, like her life.

The perfect wife they'd called her, the elegant hostess, the loving mother, the clever homemaker. She'd been the first to use basil, and was into coriander long before Delia Smith did the cooking series where she put it in everything. Her suppers were casual, with fun food, her dinners enviable, sophisticated creations. Rupert would never have got where he was without her, people often said. Rupert said it too. *Her* clothes set him off, she created the arena in which he could glow. But Rupert was more than *her* creation, or even *their* creation. He was so attractive with his close-cut hair, his intelligent nose, his jackets that never creased. He was warm, he was witty with her, but quieter in a crowd, allowing others to shine.

She had been the luckiest woman alive. Kit was successful in the States, and he'd be home in a couple of years, back in the London office. Perdita was the only little cloud, but she was a lovely girl really. It was only a phase.

Everything was perfect. She even coped well with Rupert dying, admittedly cocooned in numb disbelief.

She *had* coped. Until the funeral.

Si stood behind her on the terrace wearing a peach tracksuit. 'You're different this morning,' he said, looking at her like a doctor contemplating a patient.

'My daughter rang.'

'I knew it.' He held his palms up, triumphant. 'Actually, I did hear the phone.'

'I'll go to the village this morning. Find out what the shops sell.'

'Shop. Just the one.'

'I'll miss Waitrose.'

'Seen Tara?

'Not yet.'

'She'll be in touch, no doubt. Quite a dinky little totem beast, isn't she?' He sat down cross-legged on the grass. 'Time for meditation. Get orientated for the day.'

'You'll get piles sitting in the wet,' said Brigid.

'Got to be centred. Must be touching the earth.'

'The grass is soaking.'

'Perhaps you're right.' He stood up, rubbing his backside, and settled on a garden seat. 'Do you ever think your responsibility is so heavy you'll never manage?'

'I don't have too much responsibility these days.'

'I was thinking,' said Si, 'about me.'

She went inside, leaving him meditating on the bench under the sycamore tree. Occasionally a dried key floated down onto him, but he was oblivious, at peace with the world. It was difficult to think of anyone as free from responsibility as Si. Slowly, he lifted his hands and started to work his fingers once more against that extraordinary skull.

Dessi came into the kitchen in a yellow and black striped sweater. He toasted a slice of bread on the range. Disappointingly, it came out both charred and uncooked in different places.

Si sprang off the bench and ran to the kitchen clutching his head. 'A mirror, quick,' he said. He ran into the downstairs loo and tried to angle the top of his head to the glass. He couldn't see what he wanted. He came out. 'A hand mirror. Haven't you got anything, Brigid?'

'What's up?' Dessi asked.

'Hair. Hair. Look.' He thrust his head under Dessi's nose.

'There *could* be.' Dessi was not convinced.

Brigid inspected the waxen surface. The shining dome was muted, and she could make out a covering of down, like on a new baby's head. 'Yes,' she said. 'Definitely. Just a little hint. I'll get the mirror from my handbag.'

With a hand mirror, and a torch to see better, Si was mesmerized by emerging hair, like the first shoots of corn in the spring. He closed his eyes and sighed, long and contented.

'Lovely,' said Brigid. 'What a relief. Though you look distinguished in your own way.'

'It's not the having hair,' said Si. 'Don't you understand?'

Dessi brought him a plate of patchy toast. 'You'll need to feed it,' he said.

'I've *healed* my head.' Si bit the toast and spat crumbs over Dessi. 'Healed it. My hands have the power. *My* hands have done this.'

Rupert had loved toast. He cut it thick, and spread it as thick again with dark, chunky marmalade. He crunched noisily when he chewed. For such a fastidious man, he made a huge amount of noise eating toast. At first that jarred because in Rupert she was escaping slovenliness, she was getting away from dirt, the coating of greasy dust pervading her childhood.

Brigid's mother hadn't been exactly a slut; personal hygiene was not entirely neglected, though she never washed her hair until it was ready for it. She made up for deficiencies with an abundance of lipstick, nail varnish and perfume. As a result, Brigid never used much of any of these. It was the lack of cleaning and fresh flowers, and the profusion of smeary milk bottles, and lamb chop bones lingering in cooking pans that irked. Before she met Rupert, Brigid found sanctuary with Aunt Roo.

That she should do so was a paradox, because Aunt Roo's house was equally chaotic, yet Brigid loved going there. It was clean chaos, born of enthusiasms, and swerving interests, and uneven vitality. Even there, Brigid was tempted to straighten the curtains when they got looped up on the sash by the wind. She followed Aunt Roo round as she threw the most imaginative ingredients all into the same pie. The child Brigid wiped the lemon grater, rewashed the basin that still dribbled cream on the outside. This was clean, creative mess. Even as a child Brigid knew this mess grew out of a positive and life-giving energy, whereas at home, chaos was the result of laziness.

Aunt Roo wasn't married because her beloved Charlie had wasted away with a tumour on the lung when he was only twenty-two, but she seemed a wonderfully happy woman. She lived in her cottage in Northumbria, though just a bit further south than Brigid was now. She made dresses with skill and imagination for ladies who had neither, within the radius of her home, and often beyond. With her income, she planned treats, visits to other towns, once *Abroad*. Abroad was Honfleur, and the joy from that treat lasted months. Brigid never understood why Aunt Roo, at the height of her infectious happiness, sometimes cried. 'Charlie would have loved Honfleur,' she said as they sat in her garden looking at the photographs.

Rupert provided a more permanent answer. He was energetic and successful. He was alive. But he needed to live in harmony. He wanted flowers on the table, and meals at proper times. He was imaginative, but he liked pattern. Brigid found her happiness in the exquisite order of their lives.

One reason she agreed to stay at Highmoor House was to come north, to be near where Aunt Roo once lived, where Brigid was happy as a child. She needed the resonances of Aunt Roo now to mend her life.

She dressed carefully. Her first impression on the village would *not* be 'that poor woman'. The bronze silk cabled sweater sat snugly at the hips over oatmeal ski pants. She lifted the colours with a cornflour bandanna inside her shirt. Clothes helped.

The back lane to the village was narrow, and encroached by cow parsley, now gone to seed, on either side, but this way seemed quicker than going by road. Anyway, Brigid felt like the walk. She hoped it would clear her head. The path was downhill, and the ground was dry and dusty beneath the frost; sometimes her foot slipped. On either side, the grass and trees turned to bay, the grey brown kiss of foliate death. Although the sea was four miles away, she could smell the saltiness of it on the breeze against her face. Below her, the village huddled into a protecting fold of the moor, comfortable, and autonomous, a place unto itself. The big house behind her was aloof from the village, those who built it must not have cared too much for local company.

Barkwell, the village, was built in grey stone and had resisted improvements. On the sash windows set low in the walls there was no sign of double glazing. Whether the absence of modernization was due to innate good taste, poverty, or laziness, Brigid had no way of knowing. Here and there the stone was plastered and painted with a dull cream or a grey whitewash. There was only one village shop, *Bessie's*, acknowledged in uneven white paint on a blackboard above the door.

Brigid looked at her list and knew she really needed the car to get the shopping home. She'd buy lunch now and come back later. Around her was the smell of onions alongside bread, of exposed bacon on a slicer, and loose dog biscuits in a sack. There were overtones of limp cabbages. Outsize yellow scones dehydrated into a floury dust on the counter next to plastic toys. Ready-weighed balls of mince wrapped in cling film lodged in a small freezer cabinet alongside vanilla ice cream and frozen beans.

A man was reading a newspaper and two women were talking either side of the counter. If that were Bessie behind it, she didn't suit her name, being spry and angular, with eyes that not only took in Brigid, but swept round the shop appraising her stock in relation to the newcomer.

'Be with you in a mo,' she called.

The other woman turned round to stare at Brigid, large brass earring hoops perforating curtains of fading hair. She had a wide squashy nose and a full mouth in contrast to small nestling eyes. Eventually she smiled and her lips stayed full and moist, never elongating.

'You're the lady come to Highmoor House. Bessie was telling us. I'm Hilly, my dear.'

'Brigid.' She held out her hand, noting the brown skirt with an Aztec pattern round the hem, and the enveloping red-knitted cape which emphasized Hilly's rotundity. Her shopping basket was a garden trug.

'Oh.' Hilly didn't expect the formality and shook the slim fingers energetically with her fleshy ones. She pulled at the jacket sleeve of the man reading a newspaper. 'This is Aeneas, my hubby.'

He turned round and Brigid recognized the man who'd stared antagonistically into her car yesterday. He wore the same jacket, its waxed surface crazed with age. One side of the collar of his blue-check shirt was stuck untidily up under his ear, pulling his green tie off-centre with it. He was naturally thin, and his face showed the planes of the bones beneath. He was tall and quite good looking in a pared down sort of way, at odds with his dumpy wife. But his smile was fixed as if more by polite habit than pleasure in the introduction, and his eyes flickered over her briefly, the slightest acknowledgement that she stood before him trying to look friendly herself. Aeneas was detached from the mundane world of the village shop, apart from the gossip, especially distinct from the women. Momentarily the hazel eyes widened as if he recognized her from yesterday, then he switched off the light. He nodded abruptly, and turned back to the newspaper. It was impossible to tell what he was thinking. Hilly's hubby was there to carry the shopping, which Rupert would never have done.

'Are you settled in?' Hilly asked. 'It's a big place on your own.'

'I expected to be alone, but Si's turned up with a friend.'

Hilly pressed her hands to her cheeks in mock

horror. 'My dear,' she said, her eyes gleaming. 'Such a one.'

'Pleasant enough.'

'I blame them for sending him away. You'd have sorted him out, wouldn't you Aeneas? Aeneas was headmaster until he retired in the summer. Now he's writing a book.' She lowered her voice and giggled. 'Clever with it.'

Not so rustic after all, this 'hubby', thought Brigid and shuddered when she noticed the label of his jumper sticking up at the back of his collar.

'What can I get you?' Bessie fussed like an eager sparrow.

'Five pounds of potatoes, please. No, make that three.' Brigid looked in the cool box, her silver pen held lightly as she ticked her list.

'Fish fresh in today,' said Bessie waving towards a case of herrings wedged in a rusting cool box. 'Been to Seahouses myself this morning.'

'Si's a vegetarian. I'd better have some lentils. Eggs. Tomatoes. Is that cabbage the only fresh vegetable? Ah, carrots. What cheese have you got?' She wanted filo pastry, walnut oil and fresh basil, but these weren't in Bessie's line. No call, you see. Chilli powder would come in useful too. She picked up the *Daily Mail* in the absence of the *Independent* because any national newspaper was some sort of link with life as she knew it.

A small man came into the shop and tripped over her carrier bags. 'Oops. Sorry,' Brigid and the man both said. Underneath his orange anorak she spotted a clerical collar.

'Aah,' he said, placing her. 'Jan Morrow told me about you. Brigid, isn't it? Welcome. Cedric. C of E. Higher than normal but nothing extreme.'

'Hello.'

'Are you avid, tepid or void?' His husky high voice was full of pasted-on bonhomie. He smiled encouragingly, knowing a brisk approach was just what the church needed these days.

'I go to midnight mass at Christmas,' Brigid said. 'I'm not fond of hymns.'

'Some hymns are the pits. Absolutely. Give us one whirl, Brigid, that's all I ask. They say I twinkle in the pulpit.'

He picked up his newspaper, patted her cheerily on the shoulder and left. Brigid was surprised to find Hilly still lurking among the seed packets.

'Your arms will fall out of your shoulders with that lot,' she said. 'Aeneas and me'll take you back in our car.'

'No, really.'

'We're driving past Highmoor House, aren't we, dear?' Hilly insisted. 'To give Puddle a run on the moor.'

Aeneas said nothing, but he found his collar tickling his ear and was trying to tuck it away.

'I *would* be grateful,' said Brigid, looking to him for a sign it would be no trouble, but he was too busy pushing his collar out of sight.

Brigid got in beside a Shetland sheepdog, who looked at her suspiciously from the other end of the seat. 'That's Puddle. Say hello to Brigid, Puddle.' Hilly twisted round in her seat and smiled engimatically. Brigid couldn't make out whether it was with favour or reproof. When Aeneas drove off, the nervous Sheltie crept along the seat and put her cold nose against Brigid's knee. She stroked Puddle, and wished one of the cats at Highmoor House was a dog, to lend a sense of purpose to walking.

Outside Highmoor House, as Brigid got out of the car, Hilly wound down her window, clutched the top of it and whispered, 'Come and have tea this afternoon, dear. We can have a little chat. Last on the left in Wicket Lane.' Before Brigid could reply the car jerked away. As it circled the front grass, she saw that Aeneas looked furious.

'Funny she should ask you over,' said Si, later. 'She usually frightens people off, being a witch.'

After lunch Brigid drove to Berwick-upon-Tweed. It was cold, and the wind came in from the sea with a harsh bite, weather that forged the Northumbrian soul over the centuries. She found Somerfields conveniently next to the car park. She failed to find walnut oil or fresh herbs but did however locate ginger, dried yeast, anchovies and mascarpone cheese.

Driving home, the headache that started with a hangover felt worse, a dull persistent pain above her left eye. A hangover would have cleared by now. Could be a sinus or perhaps stress. Wind always made a headache worse. She wished she'd been quicker and made an excuse to avoid tea with Hilly.

Brigid found the cottage. It stood alone with a garden packed full of shrubs and plants, some flowering even at this time of year.

'Come in,' said Hilly, 'Aeneas is tutoring in Alnwick. They still value him, you see. He does these little seminars on logic and ethics. He believes they're the foundations of good education. The regular staff don't have the time. All the tests and paperwork. He loves teaching. It invigorates him.'

The front door led straight into the sitting-room,

which was crowded. There were plants everywhere snuggling with jugs and photos, corn dollies and china cats. There were embroidered chair backs, and crocheted doilies under vases. It was the decor of a previous generation. Brigid could see the old cooker through a door into the kitchen, and on hooks above it hung dozens of bunches of herbs. On a table was a clutter of jars and bowls. In one glass jug liquid was bubbling for no obvious reason. The smell of cooked plums hung in the room, heavy on the air like the scent of hawthorn.

Hilly had shifted from the ethnic earth figure she was in Bessie's shop to the mystic. She wore an ankle-length black skirt, and a long garnet sweater with an aubergine lace scarf wound round her neck. She'd pulled her frowzy hair up into a loop at the back of her head, revealing different earrings made of cream pebbles incised with inscriptions.

Brigid got a fleeting impression of the person Hilly once was, the imprint of a sensual young woman, perhaps voluptuous, even lustful. There were hints of dimensions to Hilly unimagined at the first meeting.

On a small table between two chairs in front of the fire tea was laid out, scones, a green-speckled trifle and a pot of tea. Hilly directed her with a wave of her hand.

'So you're a widow?' She spoke as soon as they sat down. 'Dock root tea, dear. Very good for the blood. Only mildly laxative so shouldn't give you any trouble.' She passed a cup of olive liquid and pointed to the scones.

'Since February.' Brigid took a scone. It was heavy and the taste of bicarb got behind her teeth.

'He was an attractive man, I'm sure.'

'Yes.'

'And devoted to you?' Hilly's only interest seemed to be buttering her scone, but her voice was deliberately casual, *too* casual to be indifferent.

'I hope so.' Brigid was wary.

'Devoted. As *we* are,' said Hilly, glancing up. 'I always said we'd marry, you know, even when he was away, among all the temptations at the university. He came back to me. I knew he would. The Durham girls were not for him. We women know things, don't we, dear?'

'I suppose so.'

'You've got children, I expect.'

'Two. Kit and Perdita.'

'My child was never born,' said Hilly sitting back in her chair.

'I'm sorry.'

'Perdita? Now how old would she be?'

'Eighteen.'

'Yes. Not yet a woman.'

'She thinks she is.'

'A maiden. Yes, just a girl. A handmaiden. She could have a wonderful opportunity. A life of purpose stretching before her.' Hilly nodded to herself, and served the trifle. There was an excess of angelica tossed about on the surface, 'I grew it myself,' said Hilly. 'A kindly plant.'

'I noticed your garden.'

'It complements my work.' Hilly's answers seemed to beg for questions.

'Yes?'

'They call me a pagan. Some in the village. I laugh at them, I do.'

'Right.' Brigid couldn't work out what was expected of her.

'They're coming round to it, you know, certain enlightened vicars. The natural laws. Our own dear Cedric has not yet veered that way. You met him in the shop. Unfortunately, Cedric is a pathetic little wimp, and he's terrified of the Bishop, so he's rigidly unreceptive. He hasn't really come out of the Roman closet yet. But he will. He will.'

Brigid sipped the dock root tea, and put the cup down. It was more like an infusion of rabbit droppings. She tried to take the taste away with the trifle. The angelica was chewy, like tough celery. 'I don't see Cedric going in for raves.'

'No, my dear. Neither do I.' Hilly giggled. Brigid laughed as well for the sake of manners, and Hilly giggled quite a bit more until she choked on a particularly tough piece of angelica.

A noisy car drew up outside, and a moment later Aeneas walked past the window looking quite lively. 'He loves his bits of teaching,' said Hilly.

He came in and glanced at Brigid sitting at the table. He saw Hilly's face, flushed with the giggle and the choke. He saw the untouched muddy tea, and the half-eaten trifle. He lifted one questioning eyebrow. The determined smile flagged, flattening out his bony face. It was as if a blind were drawn like an invisible cataract across his eyes when he had moved from his teaching world to this one. 'Good afternoon,' he said, looking uncomfortable. Hilly stretched out her hand insistently to him, and Aeneas took it briefly.

'You haven't drunk your tea,' said Hilly looking at Brigid.

'Your teas are an acquired taste,' Aeneas said. 'We can do coffee, though not freshly ground. Bessie doesn't keep beans.'

Brigid smiled apologetically at Hilly. 'I'm not feeling innovative today. Got a headache. Coffee would be lovely.'

Aeneas put the kettle on the cooker and came back. He hovered, not knowing what to do.

'An infusion of rosemary with basil. Do you a treat.' Hilly bustled into the kitchen and pulled sprigs from the bundles drying over the stove. 'Have it when you get home.'

Brigid was uncomfortable with his edginess and glanced at the newspaper on a side table. Aeneas looked too.

'Intercession,' he said. 'Three down.' One eyebrow higher than the other was quizzical.

Brigid read the clue. 'I wouldn't have got that,' she said. 'Not straight away.'

'Got to do something to while away the long winter evenings,' he said.

'*We* have the radio.' She hoped she matched his irony, echoed his mocking of the received rural image.

'Brigid will think us dull if you talk like that, Aeneas,' said Hilly. 'But we love it here together.' She put her hand on his wrist, proprietorially. Perhaps she sensed the shared joke.

The kettle boiled and Aeneas made the coffee in a jug, straining the grains through a piece of muslin.

'Looks like we're out of the ark,' said Hilly. 'Why don't you buy a machine to make coffee, Aeneas?' He passed the cup in silence.

Brigid said, 'I like it made like this. It's how the French always used to do it.' She didn't add that was how Rupert made it too.

Seeing Aeneas's eye flicker gratefully at Brigid, Hilly said, 'That's how *I* taught you to make it, isn't it, love?'

* * *

Brigid still had the headache when she got home. Her head was thumping as she prepared supper. Si sat at the table, hugging a mug of tea, touching his head from time to time to reassure himself the embryonic hair was still there.

'I'm giving you pissaladière,' she said. 'Found some black olives in Berwick.' She pushed the yeast pastry into a sandwich tin.

'*Pissa* what?'

'Posh pizza.'

'Is it vegetarian?'

'A few anchovies on the top. You'll have to pick them off.' Brigid shredded the basil and the rosemary from Hilly over the tomatoes. A pity to waste them.

Si picked up the *Daily Mail* and turned to the horoscopes. ' "A day you thought would never arrive is here at last. Wait no longer." ' Si read it out. 'You see. Written in the stars. Prophecy. It means my healing hands. Proof of the prediction. What has been predicted has happened.'

'You seem very exposed to invisible forces,' Brigid said, nodding her head towards the horoscopes. 'Horoscopes and energy and ancestors.' She arranged the black olives prettily.

'It's change, always change,' said Si. 'We recognize the changing Aquarian godhead.'

'The New Age,' said Brigid, 'is a bit of a rag bag, isn't it?'

'It's not fully defined. It needs leadership.'

Dessi came in to the room. 'I'll stoke the range for you,' he said.

'It's oil fired.'

'I'll lay the table.' He was vague as to which plates to

set out, and kept taking them out of the cupboard, and putting them back again. Admittedly, nothing was in sets that matched. Eventually he chose some green plates, a stainless steel salad bowl, and a blue gratin dish for the potatoes. Brigid's head was still thumping. She'd taken two Anadin.

Si said, 'You've got a headache.'

'How do you know?'

'I can see it. Your etheric web is badly tangled. Come and sit down.'

'I'm putting on the olives.'

'Put the olives down. Wipe your hands. Sit down here.' Si stood small and commanding. Had he been in the army, he'd never need raise his voice to command men, despite his height. He had a natural presence.

Brigid put the olive she was holding back in the jar and washed her hands. Meekly, she went round the table and sat on a chair wondering why she was so compliant.

'It's always soothing to have your neck massaged,' said Brigid.

'No massage. Sit up straight. Drop your shoulders.'

Rupert used to do her neck when she was tense. Then, of course, there'd been the power of love. The power of *her* love had taken comfort in the feel of his hands kneading the muscles, touching her. There was nothing personal about this encounter with Si.

Si stood behind her, and put one hand on her forehead, and the other on the nape of her neck. At first his fingers were cool and remote. She was scarcely aware of his touch. It was about thirty seconds before she felt the heat. Gradually, warmth spread across her brow, through her head, through her mind, and down to the back of her neck. She was aware her head was in the pathway between his two hands. There was a flow of benevolence between them.

Si stood back and took his hands away from her. 'Well?'

'It's gone.' Brigid moved her head about. 'It's quite gone. Completely.'

'I've done it,' he said, and thrust a clenched fist into the air. 'I'm a healer. Brigid, me old darlin'. Dessi. You're looking at a man who can heal. Two in a day. Wow. Bloody hell. I knew I could do it. I *knew* it.'

'You've found the power, Si. Fan*tas*tic.'

'We all had it once. I mean, in the Bible, it wasn't just Jesus doing miracles. All the other Messiahs were at it all the time.'

'Matthew 24, verse 24,' said Dessi. 'False prophets will appear and they will perform great miracles.'

'Impressive,' said Brigid, 'or are you making that up?'

Dessi shrugged his shoulders.

'He's a storehouse, that man,' said Si, and thumped the table with his fist, several times.

Brigid unpeeled the lattice of anchovies off one half of the pissaladière, and left it vegetarian. It was the least she could do.

Winter Solstice

The winter solstice falls on December 21st. It is a further three days before the interval of light manifestly grows longer. To the Celts the solstice extended until the sun made its obvious change in direction on the 24th. The evening of that date was the start of the day we now call Christmas day. The Jews, like the Celts, started their day at sundown, hence the importance of Friday night for the Jewish people, and the importance given to Christmas eve.

There was a pagan nativity long before the birth of Christ when the sun god was reborn of a virgin at midnight and it became apparent the sun would return again to earth. The Celts decorated their homes with evergreen to show eternal life, and with candles to encourage the sun from its lowest point, and with holy mistletoe and baked fruits to ensure the next harvest. Later, the Romans concluded their festival of Saturnalia with a feast on the day of Natalis Solis Invicti, *or the birthday of the unconquered sun. The great Persian sun god Mithras was celebrated on the same day at midnight when white-robed priests attended the altars, the smell of incense wafting all around them. Pagan festivals coincided with the Jewish celebration of the feast of lights or Hanukkah on that same day. Hence much of the present-day rituals of Christmas have their origins in the pagan world, and the date itself drew upon its Jewish roots for the date chosen to celebrate the birth of Christ.*

Having moved away from the natural rhythms of the

earth in their spiritual quest, men became deferential to religious authority, with its useful social and emotional restraints, and its comforting certainty, at the expense of inspiration from the spirit within themselves. They devote themselves to a rigid form in liturgy and concept, rather than accepting the Aquarian principle, which was also the Celtic path, that there is eternal change and renewal. It is significant the Hebrew writers should have cast the serpent, so fluid in its progress, as evil, when it was to other faiths a symbol of restoration. The serpent could slough off its old skin and emerge as if new once more.

The festivals such as the solstice fires served to create healing energy, manifested in joy and in love. Participating in them, men became aware of the resonances between themselves and the vibration and rhythms of Gaia, which was the spirit of the earth.

The Celtic Way, A.B.W.

Autumn progressed. The sky became greyer, the wind chillier. Life at Highmoor House settled into a routine. Brigid worked hard clearing up the chaos of Jan's lifestyle. She sorted the back porch, and even dared to throw away two broken umbrellas whose spokes and fabric were beyond reclaim. She stacked up the bats and racquets in a pile in one corner. There seemed no neat place for the surfboard, which stuck out across the other equipment like an angry trap. Eventually she put it up on end against the wall.

She cleaned all the rooms, pulling down cobwebs, lifting the smudges from windows, polishing the furniture. It was satisfying to see the shine come back, a deep auburn light in the mahogany. She polished harder than she need, washed heavy curtains and washed them again because they still smelled. She was frantic to get exhausted so she could sleep at nights, instead of lying awake, thinking. It suited her purpose to run round after Si, who never bothered to make his own bed. It usefully took up time to peel extra potatoes. Her tranquil mouth took on a harder line, and she could feel the furrow of a frown between her eyebrows. She'd never felt bitter like this, even about her mother's lack of parenting. But she went less and less to her room for a comforting cry. Instead she pumped more caffeine.

At the beginning of December she bought a brick-red check cloth for the table in the kitchen and the room took on a warmer ambience. She planted geraniums into pots from the urns in the garden, previously part of Philip's patriotic red, white and blue theme, and stood them on the kitchen windowsill. She hung herbs that Hilly gave her over the range to dry, and they scented the kitchen with sage, thyme and rosemary. She battled to impose an order and a beauty on the unreceptive surface of Jan Morrow's taste. Brigid made more efficient shopping trips into Berwick-upon-Tweed, and walked down to the village each day only to buy a newspaper. She went early to avoid local people, even Aeneas and Hilly. She wasn't sufficiently a real person yet to mix with strangers.

Brigid thought quite a lot of the time about the Northumbria of Aunt Roo. She had a cottage just south of Hadrian's wall. It always seemed to be summer when she visited. Aunt Roo once took her to see the nearest bit of the historic ruin, a modest relic, now only knee high at that point. Aunt Roo told stories of the civilized Romans repelling the wild men of the Borders and Scotland, and Brigid felt safe and protected on the southern side of the wall. Other days, they climbed over the dividing stones, although they could just as easily have walked round them. Once on the northern aspect Aunt Roo told tales of the brave and romantic Celts fending off the cruel Roman invaders. 'Celts, like myself,' explained Aunt Roo, 'we're from a wilder shore.' Brigid felt proud to be standing alongside her Celtic and wild aunt. Wildness was a quality she lacked, a vacancy in her blood. Aunt Roo was definitely at her best on the Celtic side of the stones, her home of the heart. Wherever Brigid stood with Aunt Roo there was a comforting orientation. Their position was always justifiable. Wildness was justified, and she very much wished she had more of it. It seemed to be a guide to the heart, especially when Aunt Roo smiled out at the far northerly Cheviot hills and whispered, 'Oh, Charlie.'

Staying with Aunt Roo coloured her understanding of geography and history throughout school. The focus had always been off centre but poised, an equilibrium of oppositions, a greater weight balanced by a longer arm. When Jan Morrow talked of Northumbria, Brigid knew immediately that was where she might be healed. If only Aunt Roo hadn't had a penchant for nightcaps of brandy beginning quite early in the evening, she might still have been there to bring sanity to Brigid's life.

Si's hair grew nicely in a hazy halo. His threatened followers hadn't yet shown up, and he spent much of the day reading. Sometimes he was with Hindu scriptures, other times he sat and stared at Egyptian hieroglyphics. On a particularly overcast morning he sat quietly with the Loeb edition of Hippocrates. On one page was the original Greek, and on the other, the English translation by W. H. S. Jones. It gave him a deceptive sense of original study. Dessi read a western, which was as far as he'd got with getting his mind together.

The concentration span was not long for either of them. Dessi fell asleep. Si was prone to doodling. With a soft pencil, on a plain sheet of unreceptive A4, Si drew a man on a camel. The flow of the man's robes echoed the shapes of the desert hills around hm, and all the movement of the lines culminated in a single stone building, a well, in the distance to the right. It expressed freedom and yearning, and the nomadic spirit of the Arab.

'That's good.' Brigid looked over his shoulder.

'I wanted to go to art college. Philip wouldn't come up with the dosh, and he's so filthy rich I'd never have got a grant I could live on. There was also an insufficiency of A levels.'

'You could be a mature student now. Nothing would depend on your background or exams.'

Si shrugged his shoulders. 'I begged him, but he wouldn't listen. Said art school was for poufters. He wanted me to go into the business.' Philip was a man who considered anything to do with the imagination effeminate.

'You're not cut out for commerce,' said Brigid.

'Now my energy is channelled elsewhere.' Si leaned back against the chair, looking the opposite of dynamic.

'I think,' said Si at breakfast the next week, 'it's time to make a move. *Progress.* Dessi?' He glanced at Tara, who sat on top of one of the orange wall units above their heads. Her eyes were full yellow-green lights, not slits any more. She blinked slowly, disdainful and cold, but intense.

'She's beaming down vibrations,' said Dessi.

Si sat cross-legged on the bentwood chair. He stared out, trance-like, across the garden. 'Almost cometh the midwinter solstice,' he said. He wore his sap green robe as he felt especially spiritual that day. Because it was cold he had his father's gardening mac, a garment better suited for flashing, on over the top. The light from the window centred its white energy upon him. A funny little fellow on a kitchen chair, thought Brigid, she'd miss him if he left after Christmas.

'Stay till after Christmas,' she said, surprising herself. 'You won't like Christmas in the van.'

'When I say move,' explained Si, 'I don't mean shift. Something should come to pass with what I'm at. A happening.'

'Ah.'

'Right,' said Dessi, and his face lit with yearning.

It was almost Christmas when Perdita finally agreed to come to Northumbria. Brigid felt a wave of gratitude and hoped it wasn't out of a sense of duty. She and this now foreign particle of herself would unite in their first Christmas without Rupert. She attacked Christmas cooking with the same energy she'd put into cleaning. She searched diligently for vegetarian suet for the pudding and mincemeat to accommodate Si. He wouldn't know the difference, it was a matter of principle not to cheat.

While she was buying sultanas locally because she'd miscalculated, Bessie said, 'Hilly isn't well.' She spoke quietly and nodded in a knowing way, as if Brigid should know what was wrong with Hilly. 'It started two years ago,' she added grudgingly, her robin-bright eyes watching her customer. Bessie came of an older community where some subjects are never framed in words. These subjects were to do with death and sorrow, but didn't include sex, scandal or money.

Leaving the shop, she spotted Dessi talking to the vicar outside the pub. She hadn't been to church, and since Cedric might now bring up the subject of midnight mass, Brigid turned abruptly for home.

'A solstice bonfire?' Cedric paused, his eyebrows shooting up and down. 'That's a jape we've never considered.'

'Being a rural community . . .' Dessi prompted.

'Great thinking,' said Cedric, 'but we must stick to fundamentals.'

'Can't get more fundamental than nature.' Dessi's wide brown eyes were curiously innocent. He lacked the guile that made the vicar suspicious of Si.

'Quite a jolly ruse to get the flock sniffing round. They're spiritually constipated, you know.' Cedric giggled. 'Overkeen on hymns with a carnal beat. They drink too much at harvest supper.'

'You'd get quite a crowd to this,' said Dessi.

'Yah. Especially as at Guy Fawkes it rained and we cooked sausages at the vicarage. They found the chip fryer. Not in the proper spirit. The lady wife had little sympathy.'

'Guy Fawkes?'

'The verger's idea. A rotten one, as it turned out.'

'That's not spiritual. Not like a solstice. Guy Fawkes wasn't getting down to the natural seasons and all that, was he?'

'Certainly not. Right, young man. That's what we'll do.' Cedric punched him jovially on the shoulder. 'An act of community and fellowship. I'll lay on coffee.'

Dessi came back from walking to clear his head. His eyes were more focused than Brigid had yet seen them. He rubbed the palms of his hands together, not with cold, but with satisfaction. 'I've been talking to the Vicar.'

'Traitor.'

'He's got a captive audience, right?'

'Only when they're glued down to the pews. We don't go into places like that, Dessi. Imagine the vibrations.'

'Not only in church. He gets people together like. In other places too.'

'Wembley stadium?'

'In the village. I've fixed it. A solstice bonfire. *He'll* get them there and then you take over. We didn't discuss the later stages.'

'The man's a vicar, Dessi. He'll get overwrought. What's a vicar doing getting involved in a bonfire to encourage the sun god to return to the earth? Is the poor man awash in the sea of faith?'

'He probably got hold of the wrong end of the stick,' said Dessi. 'Perhaps I wasn't at my articulate best. But he'll get people out there. That's the idea.'

'Could be what I'm looking for, Dessi. A platform,' Si nodded.

'He's a bit keen on being in charge. Calls it an act of community and fellowship. He's bringing coffee. I'm thinking of something more transportive.'

'What if he gets the choir in on the act? They'll drown us out.'

'You will be polite to him, won't you?' Dessi said. 'I feel guilty now about getting his hopes up.'

Si was all for wearing his sap green caftan, but Brigid pointed out it was far too cold. Instead he looked conspicuous in a turquoise boiler suit with extra layers beneath, and dark glasses. His hair now stood up from his head like a hedgehog. The soft punky spikes gave him an innocent baby-like charm. He took along his guitar. Dessi was a foil in an anorak beneath a khaki officer's coat which belonged to Philip, who seemed to have an array of outer apparel. The coat now bulged, pregnant with the anorak. He had a black all-enveloping rasta hat and carried a stained tambourine with two bells missing. None of Si's charisma rubbed off on to Dessi.

They went down the track to the village. 'You two carry on,' Brigid said. 'I'm going across to visit Hilly.' She struck off left up the lane towards their cottage.

To the side of Aeneas and Hilly's cottage was a patch of land, not exactly a field, nor was it a spinney. It was a small patch of scrub with five oaks growing in it. Brigid was about to walk past, when she spotted a figure moving among the trees. Then she saw the small fire and the flickering candles.

Brigid resisted the instinct to run to the safety of the cottage, but stood trying to make out who was there. She moved into the shadow of the cottage and kept behind a tree, closer but hidden. After a moment she saw the figure was Hilly, hampered by a long dark cloak, heavy and all enveloping. Hilly wasn't walking purposefully, as if looking for the cat or firewood, but there was a pattern to her movement. She wafted through the trees as if part of a dance, moving only within a prescribed area, a circle. She carried a flat piece of wood in one hand and moved around the small fire from which came a strong smell of different woods, not all of them sweet. The candles burned at cardinal points. Brigid knew the directions because Hilly said the cottage faced due south.

Hilly drifted from one to the other, pausing by each and murmuring softly to herself. She stood equidistant between the candles, cupped her hands to her mouth, making a piping sound like a horn. Down in the valley several dogs barked, lonely, as if at the moon. Hilly stood motionless, as if she expected more.

She turned to the side of the circle and Brigid noticed a large shallow dish glinting with water. Hilly knelt beside it and held up her arms to the sky. She made movements as if she were hauling down ropes from the sky, pulling something into her arms. At that moment the moon came out from the clouds and was reflected in the water in the bowl. It was as if Hilly had drawn the moon down to her. She bowed to the moon in the water, then as the clouds took back the mystical disc, she bathed her face in the bowl.

Brigid shivered, not only with the cold; there was a wind coming off the hills that momentarily buffeted her. She wondered whether to go to the cottage. If she did, Aeneas would guess she'd seen Hilly. He would be embarrassed. Hilly stretched out her arms, becoming, in the folds of the abundant cloak, like a huge dark crow, with menacing wings. Then – and Brigid never knew whether she imagined it – Hilly lifted up off the ground and hovered momentarily above the earth, like a primeval bird, powerful and ominous.

The wind off the moor subsided, and so did Hilly. The powerful tension caved in, and she slowly collapsed to her knees. Her shoulders heaved, as if she were crying. There had been no reply to her call, apart from the baying of the dogs.

Brigid was holding her breath. She leaned against the shading tree, and touched its bark for reassurance that she was awake. It's in the power of a witch to change shape, and Hilly was working in a magic circle. She didn't dare go to comfort the crying woman. There was something Brigid couldn't understand, something strange and frightening.

Hilly stood up, and in doing so, she returned to normal. Briskly, she poured water from a bucket onto the fire, and blew out the candles. Then she gathered up her various gear and came towards the cottage. Brigid moved round the tree, hoping she wouldn't be seen; Hilly, oblivious to everything about her, went into the cottage.

Brigid waited for ten minutes before knocking at the door. She felt shaken and depressed. All around her was darkness and sorrow. Her heart ached for Rupert. Was Hilly enacting some ancient rite using enviable powers or was she off her trolley as Bessie hinted. Aeneas was tied to this woman, and she isolated them both. Si pursued his own weird path, and Dessi lurched through his life. Perdita would arrive in a few days, bringing, no doubt, further discord.

How different to Wimbledon, where she'd have decorated the tree with silken scarlet apples and gold foil pears by now, and would probably at this moment be sipping mulled wine with Murray and Jennifer at one of their many parties. She'd be planning to go to midnight mass by candlelight on Christmas eve, and would be driving out with friends to the country on Boxing day to watch the hounds meet on a village green. She might be pursuing her own weird rituals, but they were ones she understood, ones recognized by the rest of the western civilized world. They were comforting, not disturbing. She would prefer not to be challenged by questions in this part of Northumbria.

The night air was clammy on her face as she knocked on the cottage door.

'Oh,' said Aeneas. He looked tired. His brown pullover was coming apart at the bottom of the side seam. Behind him, Brigid could see Hilly sitting in a chair staring vacantly into space, still in her huge cloak.

'Sorry. Have I come at a bad time?'

Aeneas said nothing, and looked round helplessly. He was neither the rustic plodder now, nor a man come alive with teaching. He was vulnerable, as if a tide against which he'd built a dam for years had broken its banks and was about to engulf him. Hilly glanced up, feeling the cold air.

'Ask her in, you silly boy,' said Hilly, and clambered out of the chair. She stuffed her cloak into a cupboard under the stairway.

'I'm on my way to the solstice bonfire,' said Brigid. 'Si, Dessi and the vicar are doing it. An unholy alliance. I'm hoping it will get me in the mood for Christmas.'

'If you want to be festive, my dear, willow boughs can look pretty in the house. You could take in some willow.'

'You don't mean willow,' said Aeneas.

Hilly said nothing.

'I don't know where there is any willow,' said Brigid.

'Just as well,' said Aeneas.

'There'll be trouble.' Hilly returned to normal. She sniffed. 'That Simon's going to get right up Cedric's nostrils. There'll be trouble, all right. I'll fetch our coats.' She rummaged under the stairs, but it was not her huge cloak she brought out for an ordinary walk. She handed Aeneas his waxed jacket and he sank into it as into the arms of an old friend.

'Si healed my headache,' said Brigid, feeling she owed him *some* loyalty.

'Headaches get better in their own time,' said Hilly and stomped up the stairs.

'It was instant,' said Brigid. 'His baldness too. He laid his hands on his head and then there was hair.' She stood near the fire holding her coat, sage pure wool, protectively around her. She turned up the collar to cover her ears. Sage was her colour.

'You're cold,' said Aeneas.

'I took my time,' said Brigid, hesitantly. 'I should have walked quicker.'

'People don't dawdle in this weather. You've been standing about. You saw Hilly. You waited outside to give her time.' Aeneas was embarrassed.

'Yes.'

'Hilly's sick, you see, so anything which brings comfort . . .'

'Bessie said she wasn't well. That's why I called by.'

'These things come. Two years since. This time there'll be no operation.'

'I'm sorry.'

'Best not to mention it.'

Hilly came down wrapped up in a purple cape and a woolly hat that tended to rise up on her head. She had to keep grabbing it with both hands and hauling it down again. The journey up the stairs, to say nothing of her activity in the spinney, was taking its toll. She sat down. 'Just for a minute,' she whispered. 'I started to get ready for Yule this morning, and it's taken it out of me. I didn't get very far.'

'Come to us for Christmas dinner,' said Brigid without thinking. She said quickly, 'Call it Yule, or Saturnalia or whatever. Si won't have it as Christmas. Just an excuse for a decent meal really.'

'There's no need,' said Aeneas.

'We'd be delighted,' said Hilly. 'I expect you've made changes. You're that sort of woman.'

'It would be better to stay quiet,' said Aeneas.

'Please, my love.' Hilly looked up at him coyly, then turned and nodded to Brigid.

'See how you feel on the day.' Already Brigid regretted asking.

They walked into the village, towards the open space next to the church. Hilly put herself firmly between Aeneas and Brigid, and armed them along. She had a sense of urgency, as if there was so little time that even the bonfire might be over before she reached it.

The fire was near its peak, a beacon rising into the sky. It illuminated the side of the church with a satanic orange glow. Brigid wondered if the vicar had insurance payouts in mind.

It was only a small village and one in which most people went to church, for social reasons as much as spiritual. It was an alternative to the Woolpack where they met on weekdays. Not that they were irreligious. They embraced the full church calendar with regularity, a certain amount of good will, and had acceptable ethics regarding physical relationships and other potential problem areas, though the young were getting lax. They fell short in having only scant appreciation of the more subtle doctrinal points which the vicar held dear. Cedric was a fundamentalist. He knew the answers were all there in the pages of the Bible, and were open neither to discussion nor re-interpretation. He was against hallelujahs outside of hymns on account of the practice being American. He was against incense on account of that being Roman. He was against the Sea of Faith in that it overlooked God. He wasn't as keen on the solstice bonfire as Dessi imagined, but if he chose to ignore the pagan connection, it was an opportunity to spread good will, roughly in line with Harvest supper. There was not a drop of Celtic blood in Cedric's veins. He came from Croydon.

Dutifully the village turned out, though it was hard to distinguish one from the other in their anoraks fleshed out with several layers beneath, rendering men and women the same shape. Bessie, however was still the smallest and she bobbed round the groups gathering gossip which had come in since her customers' last visits to the shop. She heaved round with her a bag of potatoes; although officially a baking was not on the programme, Bessie didn't want to miss out on a sale if it suddenly turned colder and there was a need.

Brigid recognized the man who brought the post, a spasmodic service that seemed to operate like a franchise from the post office proper two villages away. Aeneas moved away to talk to him. The man was surly and Brigid suspected he only delivered when he felt like it. There were some of the fishermen who worked out of Seahouses and chose to live away from the sound of the beating surf. Dessi pointed them out, recognizing them from one of his mind-clearing walks. One came up to Aeneas, and for the first time

Brigid saw him at ease with himself, comfortable with an old friend, relaxed. It was only a moment before Hilly went over, leaned her hand on his arm, and guided him away.

A raised voice jarred the friendly murmuring. The vicar was arguing with Si. 'Certainly not,' said Cedric. 'I shall be defrocked. I publicly state I'm not a pagan. Merely a jolly clean green cleric.'

'Of course the solstice is *pagan*, but you agreed to it,' said Si. 'Agreed to everything Dessi suggested. The bonfire. The dancing. Admittedly not the lager. That shouldn't be a problem. Think of it as mead.'

'I *did not agree* to the press being here, old chap.'

'You can't call the *Northumbrian* the press,' said Dessi.

'The national press combs the local papers for incidents,' said Cedric, 'and in the absence of bonking MPs, anything out of line with vicars is news.'

'Shall we dowse the bonfire? Tell them to go home? You got these people here, remember.'

Cedric was not to be phased. 'Get rid of that journalist, and you *can* go ahead. This is a social event, a little jolly. That is final. Not pagan. Right?'

'Get rid of the press, Dessi,' said Si, with a wave of his hand.

Dessi went up to the journalist who was a sixth-form girl out for work experience. 'Fancy a drink? They don't close for fifteen minutes.' He grinned in a winning way, but remembered his rasta hat. It wasn't going to help.

'Nope.' She marked Dessi down as simple, and waited till he'd gone back to Si. She slipped into the pub by herself in search of a warming small port.

Si stood apart from the bonfire, strumming his guitar

and practising 'Blowing in the Wind'. He wasn't certain he remembered the words. He held the guitar like a lead singer, well down over the crotch, and his vowels were Americanized. His eyes were darker than ever, and the turquoise acrylic boiler suit glowed in the depths of its creases.

'We all have our cross to bear,' said Cedric, spotting Brigid. 'I've been meaning to visit, but with seven parishes . . . you know . . .'

'Please don't worry. Si's on fine form, don't you think. Quite charismatic.' The music made her mischievous.

'Not a word I like. Damages the church, charisma. So at least you've come to our little social gathering, if not to Sunday worship? Is that a move from void to tepid?' He laughed to signal the joke.

'I've come to see Si's solstice bonfire. He asked me.'

'*Our* bonfire. I hope *you're* not getting any silly pagan ideas.'

Brigid smiled enigmatically at the vicar. 'It's more spiritual than "All things bright and beautiful".' She gave her head a little shake, and her hair fell gently into shape, still showing Rolando's influence. She narrowed her eyes and almost winked at him over the collar of her coat.

'Not everyone's favourite admittedly,' Cedric swallowed. This woman looked like trouble. There was always some lonely soul out to bed the cleric. He scampered away.

Brigid smiled. She'd got out of that rather neatly. She caught Aeneas watching her. He turned away.

The vicar, with a Queen Mother wave of his hand, summoned the choir out from where they lurked in the porch for warmth. They wore white surplices over anoraks and resembled a row of seasonable snowballs.

'*Away in a–a manger, no–o crib for a bed,*
The–e little lord Jesus lay–ay down his sweet head.'

Although a relatively unobtrusive carol, the snowballs got no further than verse two. Si pulled the strap of his guitar more firmly over his shoulders and, standing so near the bonfire Brigid feared he might ignite himself, began to strum. He needed something that went faster than the carol. He looked round at the people, catching their eyes and grinning. He knew exactly what to do. He started to strum the bit of Handel's 'Water Music' that everyone knows.

It was inspired. The younger people recognized it as churchy. After all, there had been one painful Christmas when the choir had attempted the 'Messiah'. They thought Si was part of the official plan. Admittedly, without the fifty or so instruments on a barge that had been there on its first performance, and even without the range of an organ, a guitar can sound limited, but Si plonked out the chords, moving his shoulders, swinging his hips. He maximized. Handel would have been proud. The beat spoke directly to their feet, and they began to tap their heavy boots and trainers in time with Si. Besides it was cold and they needed to keep moving. Si waved Dessi forward with his tambourine. He leaped about waving it, and though having a flawed sense of rhythm, managed to look dynamic.

Aeneas was now standing behind Brigid, though staring more intently at Si.

'Why's he playing that?' she asked. 'I wouldn't have thought he liked anything classical.'

'Water,' said Aeneas. 'The age of Aquarius. The New age. The element of fluidity.'

Rather than entertain an audience which was bouncing up and down to another rhythm, the choir, as one, ground to a halt and repaired to the church porch in a huff.

Now he had his audience, Si moved on. He slid out of 'Water Music' and into his own compulsive beat. He vocalized, halfway between a hum and a la, an Irish sound, a Celtic sound, full of sadness. Its roots were in the folk music of the north, and Ireland, and even in the searching of the American pioneers. It was the free song of the nomad, the cry of the homeless. It checked the chatter of the crowd and made them aware of their inner pain. On a cold night it was a good rhythm for foot tapping.

Dessi, sensing there was no room here for his tambourine, went to the Woolpack in case the female journalist was feeling friendlier.

From time to time Si took one hand off the strings, and waved, encouraging the people to be more responsive. One by one, self-consciously at first, they answered him, until there was a mass of about twenty-five people not merely swaying or tapping, but strutting, and swooping in time to the slow persuasive chords. They waved their arms in the air, imitating trees in the wind. They swung their shoulders down, hands sweeping the ground, and making soft moaning sounds. They weren't singing with their minds but with their hearts. Even the fidgety Bessie recognized her ancient roots and allowed herself to be sucked into the communal pulsation.

Si's face was lit from the light of the flames – and with his own exultation. For the first time he felt his power. He recognized the moment of the inauguration of his mission.

Brigid stood apart. Although she wasn't swept up in the frenzy, she swayed gently, wondering what exactly to make of Simon Morrow.

Aeneas standing behind her, explained 'The bonfire's an encouragement for the sun to be reborn after the winter. The dance helps channel the energies of the earth. There's a link between the spirits of the earth and the people. Health and fertility will result.' His voice, soft behind her, was like a sane translator of a bizarre theatre. He understood the strands which men wove into their religions, and could make sense of the pattern.

Only Hilly was unmoved. Her full mouth was turned down, her small eyes vicious. 'A thief in the night. Has that man ever had earth under his fingernails? Does he smell the new shoots before they show? What a poseur. Come Aeneas, love. We're leaving.' She leaned heavily on his arm, exhausted by her outburst, and turned away from the flames.

'Take it easy, Hilly,' he said gently as they moved away.

Brigid felt more solitary as she watched them go, and closed her eyes against the chill of her situation.

Si was in his element. He threw the guitar to the ground, and was inspiring the crowd, his turquoise track suit reflecting strange colours in the firelight. He'd taken off a few underneath layers and was quite a normal shape. His sense of rhythm was superb as he strutted before his audience. The flames leaped higher with the encourgement. Now all moved to his dance, one way, then the other, swaying, swishing down, stretching up. His eyes were closed, and he seemed apart, even from those who followed his movements so closely. Brigid could see that his power over a handful of people elated him, made him come alive.

Abruptly he stopped. He held out his hands to still the crowd. Behind him the flames leapt towards the sky. His face was tilted upwards, then slowly he brought his stare back to the people. He was about to speak. The village stared back at him with trance-like expectation.

'Know.' He spoke slowly, his dark eyes sliding across the faces in front of him, speaking personally to each, enveloping, including them all. 'Recognize.' He nodded deliberately, scanning the crowd once more. 'We are one collective spirit.'

The village stared at him, trying to get its minds round what the hell he was on about. It sounded persuasive. He sounded sane. He was a lot livelier than the vicar.

'We are one with the goddess Earth.' Si raised his hands, but with the palms down to indicate the link. 'One with all living things.'

There was an embarrassed shuffling of feet. You could lose yourself while there was music and dancing. It was different when someone spoke straight out. They didn't much go for the idea their individual souls were somehow all stuck together. Certainly not gummed onto nature.

'Feel the positive energy,' Si shouted, 'as the sun turns in her path. Feel it exclude all negative forces.' He fixed Cedric with his dark coffee-bean eyes, his wide mouth in a triumphant grin.

This approach was even further outside the grasp of the village. They cast their eyes down and nudged each other for confirmation that what they were doing wasn't daft.

Healing energy. Joy. Love. It fluttered like a flame from Si, briefly through those before him, then it was dowsed. But for one glorious moment it had been among them.

Cedric spotted the indecision of his flock and made his move. He brought the portable amplifier from the church and held a microphone in his hand. He frog-marched the choir out of the porch and gave them the beat with his free hand. The tension of embarrasment was broken by the strains of 'While Shepherds Watched'. The choir dominated by electronic volume. Almost gratefully the village returned from the unknown.

'Ladies and gentlemen,' Cedric announced, 'to conclude our little festival, linking the correctly green pastoral winter solstice to our very own Christmastide, we offer you two wonderful tableaux.'

'You what?' Si shouted. 'You fucking what?'

Cedric skipped triumphantly to the side of the church porch, and switched on a spotlight. Normally it lit up the outside of the church for midnight mass, but was not used more often because of the electric bill. He swivelled it to the left, illuminating a group of children dressed as shepherds, with teatowels on their heads, hanging on to three restive sheep and a goat with dog leads. The crowd gasped, though not in awe. 'There's our Belinda, look,' said one proud mother.

Triumphantly, Cedric swung the light in the opposite direction to reveal, beside the lychgate, three embarrassed wise men with foil and cottonwool crowns. Their camel, cut from several sides of cardboard crisp cartons, joined at painful angles by sellotape, fluttered unrealistically in the breeze.

'What the hell are you playing at?' Si shouted,

striding away from the fire. 'This is the very moment when the earth is turning from sleeping to life. Couldn't you feel the links we were getting with the spirit of the earth, you silly little man? It's a crucial, seminal moment in the year.' He strode over to the vicar, and his hands were hovering over him, as if deciding which well-padded bit to grab.

Dessi came out of the Woolpack at that moment, somewhat disappointed with his progress over a pint with the would-be journalist. He was in time to stop Si thumping the vicar.

Cedric picked up Si's guitar from the ground, keeping a wary eye on Si, and triumphantly strummed out 'Hark the Herald', striking a blow for Christianity. The would-be journalist considered whether a piece on loony clergy or on mad messiahs would best serve her literary ambitions.

Si strode away into the dark, the turquoise boiler suit shimmering all the way up the hill, with Dessi bobbing behind him, trying to find soothing words.

It took until Christmas for Si to get over his confrontation with Cedric. 'We were on the brink,' he said, 'when all those people could have realized their affinity with the earth, the stupid oaf produces a cardboard camel.'

'Cedric has his position to consider,' said Brigid. 'The newspapers do love a bit of eccentricity in the clergy. A couple of joyful leaps and they'd claim he'd had an orgasm.'

'Cedric and orgasms are mutually exclusive.'

'Why don't you stop griping and do something useful. You could pick me some holly.'

'I'm not celebrating Christmas, you know.'

'Fine by me.'

'However, bringing green boughs into the house is splendidly pagan, a symbol that the earth is still living during this barren time. Dessi, you could get some yew and some ivy at the same time.'

Dessi dug up the fir tree which he could see was brought in each year by the piece of tinsel still clinging to one branch. He carried it into the house singing 'Deck the hall with boughs of holly'.

'Cut that crap for a start,' said Si. 'The last thing we want is carols. You're not the vicar.'

Brigid found some baubles in the boxroom on the top floor, but they looked thirty years old and she put them back. Instead she bought five metres of red ribbon from Bessie, who measured in yards, and collected pine cones from the spinney above the village. She put whole branches of yew on the window sills and gave them more berries of marzipan dyed red with food colouring. Jan was happy to dye her food all sorts of colours, judging by the number of small bottles Brigid found in the pantry. She bought extra large cream candles and put them in the windows to light on Christmas night, to show there was light and life and energy in the house.

She wasn't looking forward to this first Christmas without Rupert, but she was eager to make it go well, then get it behind her. Dessi wasn't certain whether he should celebrate Christmas or not. He was excited. He found the tarnished tinsel Brigid had consigned to the waste bin and festooned it over the tree, cancelling out the impact of the simple red bows and cones. 'There,' he said, eyes wide with wonder, and Brigid didn't have the heart to take it down.

'We'll have Christmas dinner in the dining-room,'

she said, determined, although her regime of regular ventilation through the house had failed to dislodge the musty, damp smell lingering.

'It's arctic in there.' Si was hunched up against the kitchen range.

'We'll do it properly,' said Brigid. This was another challenge, another means of getting through her life. So she cleaned the dining-room. It was, as in most Victorian houses, unnecessarily large, and was at one with the outsize original, ostentatious furniture. The mahogany table, without its extension leaf, seated twelve. The Victorian Chippendale chairs around it were heavy and the seats covered in maroon velvet, from which it was difficult to brush the grey bloom of dust. The sideboard was magnificently carved, though of tank-like proportions. It would dwarf the turkey. At least Aeneas would be there to carve. Si would refuse to touch it, Dessi would hack it into chunks.

She found a huge white cloth in a linen chest on the landing. She swagged ivy round the edges of it and at strategic points along the table. There was mottled silver cutlery in the gloomy depths of the sideboard, and crystal glass dulled by a greasy mist.

She and Rupert had vied in their decorations, in the trimmings, in the flowers for the table. Rivals, and yet sharing. Everything Rupert created brought her pleasure. His eye for colour and line was as good as her own and, because he was a man, complementary.

Dessi produced some wind chimes, a construction of metal tubes and a disk carrying the face of the laughing sun. When a breeze caught the disk, a piece of wood knocked against the tubes. The sound was gentle, a random series of closely related notes. It might get annoying in time. He hung it in front of the sash window. The draught flowing between the ill-fitting frames caught the chimes and they sang out, quite merry for the time of year.

'They bring positive energy to the place,' explained Dessi, 'the energy of the wind turned into music.'

Brigid carried in wood, and stacked it by the fire-place. She made a faggot of crumpled newspaper and lit it beneath a mound of twigs, cursing herself for not getting wood and firelighters from Bessie. She nursed the fire through the first difficult stages, using a news-paper to draw up the flames. This room would need a good twenty-four hours to begin to warm up. The fire-place had forgotten how to function. It was like getting a baby to eat solids. She did the same for the fire in the sitting-room. They were moving out of their kitchen phase, Christmas was going to be exemplary. All she need do was keep a firm hold on fabrication. She must pretend everything was fine.

At seven in the evening of Christmas eve Perdita arrived in her car. It was old, but looked older because of Perdita's lack of concern for it. She blasted on the horn and emerged energetically. There seemed to be yards of orange legging unfolding from under the steering wheel. Si, who was morosely staring out of his bedroom window at the time, perked up. He'd sup-posed Perdita would be a younger version of Brigid, and so to his mind, veering towards the prim. Happily, orange leggings could never be demure. He went downstairs.

'I'm here,' Perdita yelled at the front door, being too laden to ring the bell, and too lazy to free a hand to do so. She wore an extravagantly fake fur bomber jacket of soft blue, the hairs gummed together in unhealthy tufts. Her tartan mini skirt clashed with the leggings, and the brim of her baseball hat yawned upwards in an iridescent white sphere. She stood tall and aggressive, one side of her mouth pouting, the other curved up in a smile.

Brigid heard the car and ran to the door. She opened her arms, closed her eyes against the details, and hugged her daughter with all the love accumulated since she'd last seen her. It's the way of mothers. Perdita extravagantly and noisily kissed Brigid's nose.

'No Jez?'

'That ratbag? Not likely. It's so *wonderful* to be free of men. Fan*tas*tic.' She stood back to look round. 'Bit of a pile, this.'

'Welcome.' Si stood calm and important in the back of the hall. He held out one hand, forcing her to walk across the black and white tiles to him. Perdita walked, not out of courtesy, but because she was thinking what a weird guy this was. She looked at him from above, and marvelled at the length of his eyelashes and the curious downy hair sprouting all over his scalp.

Unconcerned by her appraisal, Si smiled with only his eyes, not a muscle of his full mouth moving. Brigid hadn't considered how Si might behave with girls. She saw most men would envy his charismatic silence, not pity his lack of inches. His confidence was thrown into relief by Dessi, who came into the hall after brushing the cats. He tentatively sniffed his hand before offering it to Perdita. His limited vocabulary deserted him and his tongue flickered nervously over his top lip.

Later, in the brighter light of the kitchen, Perdita didn't warm to Si. She thought his hair looked mangy, for a start. It was a misjudgement for him to put on his sap green caftan after supper and play sad music with his guitar, sitting on the kitchen table. He felt he needed to dispel the bad vibrations brought on by Brigid's Christmas preparations. The caftan often had an excellent effect on girls more easily impressed than Perdita, girls who were eager to *live* but not capable of it on their own. The usual speculation of what he was wearing underneath, and what that might mean, was lost on Perdita. Her pulse rate was more usually raised with the thump of heavy metal, she meant *really* heavy, you know?

'I like orange,' said Dessi, looking at her leggings.

'You keep your paws off them,' said Perdita.

On Christmas morning Brigid gave Perdita a cheque, but her real present of love was a cat cushion, a lavender cat with quilted flowers on his chest, and eyes of pale green glass, wide and loving. It was useless and strange but beautiful. She hoped Perdita would appreciate it.

'I like that,' Perdita said, morosely hugging the fabric cat to her. She wore a black tube of a dress which came down to her ankles. Instead of the streetwise urchin of yesterday, she was a forlorn waif from the same sort of street. 'I'll have to get back tomorrow,' she said only a few moments after. 'I'm not made for the country.' Later, she put the fabric cat beside the furry lump sleeping by the range that was Tara and Tiberius. They scrapped over him and tore out one of his green glass eyes.

Si handed out pagan gifts. There was a book of Runes for Brigid, and a packet of condoms decorated with suns for Perdita. He'd bought them earlier in the week with a view to shocking a prim daughter, but he wished he'd thought of something more sophisticated.

Perdita wasn't exactly classy, but she'd know sophistication when she came across it. Jokes about condoms are invariably childish. He forgot to get anything for Dessi.

Perdita gave everyone incense burners. She found them useful herself, not for spiritual purposes, but for covering up smells.

Brigid neatened up the Brussels, marking each base with the sign of the cross, that it might get cooked through. They were excellent Brussels, small and bright green. They symbolized her old life, clean and fresh, lying orderly and controlled in the colander. Rupert loved to cook with her, and he was adventurous. He would toss spring onions on scrambled eggs, chocolate into a chicken stew, Mexican style. No-one could have a husband who was such fun in the kitchen. No-one could have a husband who was such *fun*.

The Christmas before last he had brought home oyster mushrooms to put in the stuffing. Perdita was out with friends and they'd got rather drunk over supper. Brigid sat on the floor in front of the fire. She could remember she wore a crêpe silk shirt in a soft willow green. It suited her. Rupert sat on the floor, too, a little way apart, leaning back against the sofa.

'Oyster mushrooms,' she said, 'aren't they an aphrodisiac?' She undid the two top buttons of her silk shirt, and looked up at Rupert with one eyebrow raised, half laughing.

'Not mushrooms,' he said, standing up. 'Only oysters, I believe.' He walked over to the table behind the sofa where they'd put their Christmas presents, and picked up the novel Perdita had given him. He sat on the sofa and began to read it.

Brigid, as she now finished washing the Brussels, remembered thinking as she buttoned up her shirt, how devastated she'd feel if Rupert had another woman. She realized, of course, that the wine, instead of making him amorous, merely made him unobservant. She never felt alluring in that shirt again.

There was another ripple last Christmas, which had uncharacteristically flawed the tranquillity. His sister gave him a shirt, a good shirt with an exquisite collar and stiff white cuffs. 'Those cufflinks I gave you three years ago would be just right with that,' she said, and went upstairs to find them. Looking in the drawer where he kept handkerchiefs and studs, she came across another pair of cufflinks, chunky gold, with a single letter on each. It might have been an S or it might have been an old fashioned J. Either way, they seemed to have nothing to do with Rupert. She couldn't explain why later she never asked about them, but put them away at the back of the drawer, behind an unused gift-packed bottle of after-shave.

Brigid tested the temperature of the dining-room. The fire hadn't made much impact. Outside, frost tried to be festive, in the absence of snow. The grass below the window was crisp and solidified. In the distance, a heavy foggy mist hung over the valley, seeming to cut the village off just as surely as a heavy snow would have done. Through the mist a car was coming into focus, materializing out of the smoky fog like a clever bit of filming. It was Hilly and Aeneas. They parked and made their way round to the kitchen door. Hilly, holding Aeneas's hand, looked bent and frail, wincing as she moved.

'Just made it,' said Hilly. She was wearing her large enveloping cape, the one she used in the spinney. Brigid hoped that was for its extra warmth. She didn't want any shape-changing today.

Aeneas looked tidied up and uncomfortable. He gave Brigid some white hellebores, pink-tinged and reluctant to open their petals fully like sleepy babies. 'From the garden.' He no longer looked vulnerable, but back in his detached blank look.

Brigid put them on the table, and they made the ivy come to life. 'Just right,' she said.

Hilly was scrabbling through the inner pockets of her cloak, of which there were many. She took specs from one. She flourished a large bunch of mistletoe, conjuror-like. 'Not the presents, of course, just an offering. Off my baby oak.'

Si was frustrated. This was orgy time. Playing charismatic with Perdita wasn't paying off. She was acting dead. Si grabbed the mistletoe and, holding it over Brigid's head, kissed her on the mouth. He needed to shock. Brigid could taste whisky on his lips. She was embarrassed. Si realized that and waved the bunch over Perdita and Hilly and kissed them each with the same extravagance, which cleared the air. Hilly said 'Oh,' and squirmed. Perdita laughed out loud, and not especially with pleasure. Si scowled at her. Dessi leaned against the range and looked wistful.

'The berries are pale, and so pertain to the moon,' said Hilly, taking no further notice of Si. 'This plant is of the feminine element. The polarity of the berries changes in tune with the menstrual cycle, and its juice is like semen, just as the feminine contains the male. There is no more powerful plant.' She was out of breath and sat down, but her eyes were on Perdita.

'No more powerful plant,' repeated Dessi, his eyes especially wide today.

Hilly caught her breath and started to cough. Aeneas held her back where it was hurting, and the expression on his face was of total detachment. Then he leaned over and asked, 'Do you need some water?'

'What you need is a Yellow Parrot,' said Si. 'We all do. I've got the recipe.' He fetched bottles from the trolley in the sitting-room and sloshed together absinthe and apricot brandy. Brigid averted her eyes.

They sat shivering round the dining-table while Aeneas carved the turkey. The wind chimes were active, and since they had a bell-like quality, quite seasonal.

'I'm glad to meet you at last, Perdita,' said Hilly. 'You've been much on my mind.'

'What?'

'My child would have been a daughter.' She stared intensely across the table.

'Oh, right.' Perdita turned to look at Si, fractionally widening her eyes, asking where's Mum got this one from? Si was splashing wine into all the glasses, red and white for all, and stuffing cashew nuts into his mouth with the other hand.

Dessi fulfilled the role of a revolving hotplate in a Chinese restaurant. 'Brussels? Potatoes? Parsnips? Courgettes, Perdita?'

'You've been to a lot of trouble,' said Aeneas staring at the roast potatoes with rosemary and the parsnips glazed with redcurrant.

'A *little* profligate,' Hilly whispered to Aeneas.

'I just wanted the meal to be different,' Brigid found herself apologizing.

'It is.' Si was proud Brigid had gone to trouble for him. The mushroom and chestnut coulibiac, decorated with pastry scales, was breathing steam on the serving dish before him, akin to a ladylike dragon.

'What does that do for your sperm count?' Perdita asked, waving her fork towards it. The Yellow Parrot was provocative.

'Gives them all two tails.' Si perked up with Perdita behaving like a human being at last. 'You get a lot of wriggle.'

'I'm cold, Aeneas. Would you bring me my cloak, love? Don't be offended, Brigid. It's just silly me.'

'Not the cloak, Hilly. I'll get you my jacket.'

'The cloak, Aeneas.'

'Let me lend you a cardigan,' said Brigid. 'Not quite so heavy. I'm sorry about the fire being ineffective.'

'Aeneas is getting my cloak,' said Hilly, staring meaningfully at the stationary Aeneas.

'I'll get it,' said Dessi, eager to help.

Hilly stood up well away from the table and took the cloak. She picked it up by the collar and whirled it round her. It swished round her tubby figure clockwise, and then unwound the other way. 'Widdershins,' she whispered, smiling. The wind chimes moved up a gear. Outside the window, the weather was deteriorating, and an early dusk was settling on the afternoon.

By Aeneas's expression Brigid knew Hilly was up to no good. Once enveloped in her ceremonial regalia, Hilly took on increased presence. She pecked her food with the disinterest of the sick but every turning of her fork seemed significant.

Aeneas had a second helping of everything. Hilly frowned. She frowned even more when Brigid served the Christmas pudding into showy brandysnap tuilles and handed round a jug of vanilla sabayon. This may all be pretty grim, thought Brigid, but at least the food's OK.

'You *are* a very good cook, my dear,' Hilly said.

'I could really fancy you for this, Brigid,' said Si, looking at Perdita.

'Portents fruitfulness,' said Hilly. She looked down at her pudding without picking up her fork, as if to eat it would destroy the symbolic power.

'It's bloody cold in here,' said Perdita. She fetched Brigid's shawl, bought in Berwick for protection on Northumbrian winter evenings and wrapped it round herself so it came half way up her face like a yashmak. She looked out over the top with half-closed, speculative eyes and Si wondered why women of the East ever thought it was some sort of protection. It reminded him of India.

'India's not the answer,' he said, apparently out of the blue. 'Not the spiritual answer.'

The Yellow Parrot was slow to get into Perdita's system, but when it did, it got everywhere. She extended her shoeless foot under the table and rubbed her toe up and down Si's shin. He took no notice, beyond retracting his leg. This was more like it. Keep her panting.

Perdita was annoyed. 'When did you ever go to India then?' she demanded. India counted as living, and she hadn't done that yet. Surely this undersized mangy prat with no sensory nerves in his legs hadn't got there first.

'When I sold the bike – the Ducati. Dad didn't cough up often, but when he did, it was mega.'

'Dream speed,' said Dessi. 'The dimension of heaven. The nearest you can get on this earth.' The

Ducati had impressed him most of all, even more than Si's spiritual gifts.

'Just another boring bike,' said Perdita. 'I shall go to India soon.'

'Kashmir,' said Si. 'Lying in a boat on Lake Dal. Just me and the fishermen and the lilies.'

Hilly banged down her coffee cup. 'I want to go home,' she said. Aeneas winced at the abruptness. The wind chimes were out of control. The guiding cord from the sun disk was in a perpetual whirl. Dessi glanced up at them, frowning. Was this the result of Hilly's negative energy, or the positive natural force itself in contest with the old bat?

'Let the others finish,' Aeneas said.

'Perdita,' Si was excited, 'you ought to understand. It's a really great bike. The synthesis of the material and the spiritual. To fly on one is to exist on both planes.' He nearly added, 'Like on a broom stick.'

When Aeneas fetched his coat from the kitchen, Hilly surreptitiously drew a bottle from another pocket of her cloak. 'My seven fruits wine,' she whispered. 'It's the quince that gives it the flavour.' She tapped the side of her nose. 'My secret.' She turned to Perdita. '*You'll* like it, my dear.' Hilly was smiling as she went out of the door. Brigid wondered why Hilly'd waited until Aeneas was out of the room before giving them the bottle. Or why she'd been so keen to come in the first place and then in such a hurry to leave. She was ambivalent, sometimes wanting Brigid as a friend, and at others seeming to dislike her.

In the evening after a supper of cold pickings and salad, they retreated to the warmth of the kitchen, which felt like the heart of the house once more. Brigid was growing fond of the room. They drank Hilly's seven fruit wine. It proved to be rich and strong like drinking a liquid well-brandied Christmas pudding. Brigid had only one glass, but Perdita, Si and Dessi finished the bottle.

'I'm going up now,' mumbled Perdita, and found the door by an indirect route. Two minutes later she was back, giggling. 'Bye bye, turkey,' she gurgled. 'Bye bye, turkey, goodbye.' She disappeared from the room again and stumbled up the stairs.

Brigid went into the dining-room where she'd left the turkey under some foil, on the grounds it was colder there than in the pantry. The foil was on the floor and Tiberius stood over the carcass like his namesake at the end of an orgy. Tassie was fighting with a leg bone on the floor below. There was no third cat, but there didn't need to be.

'No more cold turkey, Dessi,' said Si. 'Lucky old you.'

Brigid slammed the door on the scene, and put off the clearing until next day. Through the cat flap came Tara, arrogant and superior to food. She stalked through the room with her eyes fixed on her destination – the door into the hall, each paw thrown down in turn with total certainty, and her tail high like a periscope.

Ten minutes later Si yawned, 'Bit tired for some reason.' Brigid was grateful she didn't hear him fall down the stairs, which seemed a possibility at the time.

Dessi leaning heavily on the kitchen table, said, 'I owe everything to Si. He rescued me, you know.' His voice was slurred, and he looked as if he were about to cry.

'Rescued you from what?'

'The hell at our school. I was the only scholarship boy. The only one without any money. Si saw to it I wasn't bullied. I'd never have got through without him.' A tear shimmered in Dessi's eye and trickled down his cheek.

'That was kind of him.'

'Not especially. He was a failure too. All he had was money. He had more than anyone. It attracted people, all the thick ones, all those who didn't do well at games. There were a lot of people like that at our school. He only had money, but it was more than I had. The money gave him a following. I was in his gang because he was kind. We made him feel he was somebody. He still needs that from me. To know I approve. That's it, you see.' Dessi stood up and now that he'd explained, seemed to lose a weight from his shoulders. Almost cheerfully he meandered over to the door, displacing several bentwood chairs on the way.

At last, at last, the dreaded Christmas day was almost over. Brigid lit a candle and put it in the centre of the kitchen table, and switched off the other lights. She sat still, watching the flame writhe and turn, flutter and flare up again. She watched it until her breathing became slow, and the weight of waiting for the day to pass diminished. She saw nothing within the flame, it told her nothing but she *felt* a peace. It was as if the candle had lit a small light in the despairing depths of her mind, passed on its essence, as Buddhists believe that life is passed on. She became someone different. Momentarily, she could detach the memory of Rupert from herself. She could look on his face. She could see that the year would turn, and that winter would become spring, although it would never be young again. The flame flickered and she watched it through half-closed eyes. It burned stronger and more ferociously. It gave the promise of the return of the sun. She opened her eyes again and the candle fell over. The red-check cloth was on fire. She was so anxious to dowse the flames she didn't hear the rhythmical thumping sound coming through the ceiling.

Perdita made a noisy escape early on Boxing day.

'Have you *got* to go?' asked Dessi, his eyes quite cow-like as they looked at her.

'I'm not staying here,' said Perdita, 'not in this dump.' She saw Brigid's face, and added, 'If it were only you here, Mum, I'd stay. It was a smashing dinner. Really.'

'It's very quiet here,' said Brigid, more to comfort herself than Perdita.

'Not quiet enough,' said Perdita. 'The place is full of weirdos. Did one of them set fire to the tablecloth or something?' She looked at the cloth on the floor in the corner, still wet and singe stains on show. There was a scorch mark on the formica.

'Just a little accident. Still, I was fond of that cloth.' Brigid put a pot of geraniums over the scorch mark.

'Shall I get Si up to say goodbye?' asked Dessi.

'Don't bother. He's not exactly sex on wheels, is he?' She went out with a small bag and most of her clothes loose over her arm. She dropped a bra on the gravel drive. Dessi stood dithering as to whether he should or shouldn't pick it up. Perdita retrieved it herself and muttered, 'Lazy cow.'

Dessi watched her battered car disappear down the hill in silence, then went to his room and stayed there all day.

* * *

'Hilly would like to see you.' On the phone, early in January, Aeneas was anxious. 'Do you mind?'

'I'll come this morning.'

'I should tell you . . . not much longer, it seems.'

'I'll come with you,' said Si.

'You weren't asked,' said Brigid. 'She's dying.'

'Exactly. And I'm a healer,' said Si. 'I can't let the opportunity slip.'

Against her better judgement, Brigid walked down the lane with Si. Neither spoke. Brigid thought about using the car, which would be quicker, but this was an old-fashioned visit to the sick, one that needed to be measured in steps of time, and to the rhythms of the land around them. There was time for the walk. Brigid appreciated Hilly's bonding with the forces of nature. They walked down the hill to the cottage, sheltering in the barren fold of the moor.

Si kept lifting his face to the sky and mouthing silent words. He stretched out his hand and touched hedgerow and grasses. 'I must find the strength,' he said.

Aeneas was waiting at the window and opened the door for them.

Hilly sat in a large winged chair by the fire, a patchwork blanket over her knees, the work of winter evenings, made with the love that should have gone into the lining of a child's crib. Beside her on a table was a half-finished mug of Ovaltine. Aeneas took it away in a gesture of tidying up. The smell lingered sweet and warm. It mingled with the smell of death in the room, the threat lurking beneath the Dettol, cologne and talc. The cells of the body had realized their end and already begun their slow decay. Puddle lay at her feet in desolation. In her sensitivity, she knew all nuances of pain and sorrow around her.

On the table at the side of her chair was a large leather purse, the type made of soft skin with a drawstring thong round the top. Something sharp was pushing the leather out on one side. Brigid wondered what was in it. Hilly never took that shopping with her.

'Started late on Boxing day,' said Aeneas, 'the bleeding. We knew Hilly had the tumour, of course, but it developed between tests. Then it was all too late. It really wasn't the hospital's fault.' Aeneas's sense of failure hung around him, as Hilly's great cloak had hung around her as she cast her spell.

Hilly'd lost weight. The face was no longer round, nor the mouth so full. 'Cis, she's the nurse, makes me get out of bed to stop clots. She's determined I'll die from what I'm meant to, not poor nursing. I could see the hills if I were still in bed.'

Si agreed. 'You should be in sight of the hills to pull strength from the earth.'

'There's not room for the chair in the bedroom.' Aeneas looked apologetic again, as if that were his fault too. 'She could move into the other bedroom.'

'No,' said Hilly, stretching out her hand to her husband, 'I want our room as it's always been.' She smiled up at him, as if safe in his loyalty and caring, yet still needing to point it out to Brigid.

Si stood squarely in front of Hilly. 'I've brought you my gift.'

She looked from his face to his hands, which were empty. 'Sorry?'

'I'm a healer.'

'Not now.' Aeneas put his hand on Si's arm. The hand was brown as summer, a clumsy hand, without elegant angles at any joint. A masculine hand lacking deception.

'I have to try. You've nothing to lose.' Si shook him off, and set his feet apart to assert his stance.

'Hilly has her own powers.' Aeneas wasn't used to being disobeyed by the young. 'I said *not now*.'

'Let him try.' Hilly's eyes grew smaller and snake-like.

Si stood behind her. He put one hand on her brow, and the other on her shoulder. He stood still, with closed eyes. He went pale with concentration.

Hilly sat with a look of resignation. Aeneas stared moodily out of the window, his face unreadable. Brigid wondered if he ever looked cross, or whether, when the weather was stormy, he merely retreated still further within himself. Si swapped hands and concentrated again. At last, he took his hands away and wiped them on the back of his jeans. He walked round the chair to look Hilly in the face.

Hilly said, 'It didn't work, did it?'

'The energy was in my hands. There was a blockage,' Si said accusingly.

'Whatever you say,' said Hilly, momentarily triumphant. 'Oh dear, I'm so tired. I wanted to talk to Brigid.' Her eyelids had a transparent look. Briefly, she opened them. 'Will Perdita have a child?' she whispered.

'I expect so. One day.'

Hilly nodded and closed her eyes. Si took the top sheet of the telephone pad and doodled with a stub of pencil. He was facing the window, and he produced his own interpretation of the hills which were out of sight in this view. The hills were realistic but there were deep shadows beneath the trees so that you knew there was bright sunshine to create them. In the foreground he had caught the sparkling dew in the cups of celandine, so real that you *knew* it would soon evaporate in the heat. There was texture on the bark of the birch just outside the window, and there were crisp knots of lavender flowers under the hedge. It was a picture for all the senses.

'Was it peaceful for *Rupert*?' Aeneas asked eventually.

'Peace didn't come into it. It was a heart attack. Instantaneous.'

'So no last words?'

'No last words.' No last words, as such, thought Brigid. Momentarily, she envied Hilly, was jealous of her for Rupert, sad that he didn't make a tidy end. What might Rupert have said if he had had the time? She would never know. Or could you say his last words were spoken at the funeral?

Si finished his drawing and put it on Hilly's knee. 'I'm off,' he said.

When Hilly woke up she didn't return quite so close to the world as before. She tried to focus on Brigid, and opened her mouth, only to shut it again. After a moment, she tried again. 'I'm sorry,' she whispered, 'I'm so sorry.'

'You've nothing to be sorry for, Hilly.'

Hilly looked down and shook her head.

'She's confused.' Aeneas picked up the leather purse from the table beside her, and put it in a drawer. Hilly looked down at the drawing Si had left, staring at it, her eyes moving over the hills and flowers. She stretched out her forefinger to touch the bark. She smiled and closed her eyes again.

* * *

Brigid made herb omelettes for supper. She thought of Rupert as she chopped thyme. He'd been such fun in the kitchen. Hadn't he? They'd laughed so much. He'd been witty. Brigid had laughed. Was it really because she was having so much fun? Or was it because their life was so carefully created, so successful, that thinking she was having fun was all a part of the creation. The *perfect* marriage. That was what other people said as if perfection was a quality on its own, not made up of anything else. Perfection. For the first time, it seemed a cold and lonely achievement. Perfection can be isolated, uncontaminated by anything else. Perfection must stand alone.

She beat the eggs, almost frantic in her search for some satisfaction in what she was doing, and flourished the pepper mill over the bowl. The butter in the pan smelled sweet and nutty, and she put her head down to inhale its essence. It brought no comfort.

The phone rang. 'It was very peaceful,' said Aeneas. 'She was looking at Si's picture. She'd looked at it most of the afternoon. It was the last thing she saw. She never said another sharp word.'

Outside the window, Brigid saw the first snow coming down, large white determined flakes. The garden was filled with the magic snowlight that can make the soul gasp at its beauty.

Brigid told Si about the drawing.

'Sometimes there's no healing.' He shook his head, amazed. 'But I gave her peace. I feel so humble. I really gave her peace.'

'That's something we'll never know,' said Brigid tartly.

Imbolc

In the Celtic world, what is now February 1st marked the end of the icy grip of winter. It was a time of the coming of milk for lambs, for all kinds of beginnings, a time of awakening and a time of new life. Now because many of the snows are still to come people behave as if it were still winter. Today we wonder that the lambs are born so early and to such harsh conditions, but the Celtic people understood the earth had turned to its renewal and they saw nothing strange. It was not yet a time for their journeys out into the world, for their renowned visits and celebrations, but a time of the home and of small pleasures.

Imbolc was associated in the Celtic calendar with the Brigid, the goddess of three forms. At Imbolc, Brigid transformed from a hag into a beautiful young girl, and because she was the mother of memory, she was a muse for poets, and the inspiration for all young men. She didn't age chronologically, but changed with the seasons, and with circumstances. She was associated with creation, for the imagination that is remembering, seeing back into the truths that were already known, and seeing them anew. Later she would become the matron who shaped the lives of others, as an enabler or even as a smith. She was the carer, and the provider; she was the epitome of womanhood. As a matron she was also the old crone who had gained the wisdom with which she was able to heal the world. That she alone could heal others made her beauty superfluous. What the world has always sought is to be healed. Brigid was the three faces of woman, and her range of empathy in mythology was wider than that of even the Virgin Mary. Today, many men carry this ideal in their hearts without ever having heard of her. She is associated with the snowdrop which often first flowers on her day.

In the sixth century, the Christians hijacked this pagan goddess and called her St Brigid of Kildare.

The Celtic Way, A.B.W.

Brigid looked at the bedroom ceiling. It was bright, reflecting the snow outside, and the clear pale sky above it. She was wakened by the pitiful cries of the new lambs in the lambing sheds of the nearest farm. She'd heard their mothers bleating in the night and buried her ears in the pillow against their pain. It was her birthday, February the first.

She made some tea in the kitchen, still in her dressing-gown, and took it back to bed. She sat hunched up under the eiderdown, and read the paperback she'd got in Berwick the previous day. Highmoor House was not a home with duvets. Brigid rather liked the white sheets and honeycomb blankets. They were more of a physical presence than the soft encompassing by air and feather.

Today she was forty-four years old. Rupert always bought her pink roses, the sort that veered towards tawny. They were expensive, being less usual than the boudoir flush found in every florists' shop. Since Perdita was unlikely to remember, there'd be no flowers today.

Right until the end Rupert was wonderful with presents and surprises of all kinds. Some people might have said that it was proof of a guilty conscience, but

Brigid knew he'd been like that from the start. From the day she met him he always had the ability to surprise. She was introduced at a party and friends were discussing going to a race meeting. 'Will *you* take *me*?' were his first words to her, face straight as an undertaker's. He surprised her until the end if she chose to see the funeral in that light.

Two weeks before he died, and only a short time after her birthday, he brought home an aqua blue vase of Hebron glass. He waited, expectant and pleased as a child while she unwrapped it. 'I knew you'd like it for the green hellebores,' he said. 'I saw it in Barnaby's window when I was passing. Blue and green. Clever together.'

'You've given me a birthday present,' said Brigid. 'Those earrings were more than enough. I love them.'

'It was there and I knew how much you'd like it,' said Rupert, simply. He pulled her to him, and held her against his shoulder, and he smelled of the air outside, cold and fresh like the sea. She was exactly the right height to snuggle the top of her head under his chin, when they stood together. 'Our minds are so close,' he whispered into her hair, 'as if we're one person.' He kissed the top of her head, and went to make some coffee, smiling and content.

She hadn't thought it strange that it was so long since they'd made love. They shared the same bed, and they wove their arms around each other in sleep, but there'd been no love-making for over a year. Not that sex was of paramount importance, *ever*. Their marriage was on another plane, spiritual, more creative and harmonious. Brigid felt at one with Rupert even to the end.

Enough of that, she thought, and climbed out of bed.

She had a bath, and wished Highmoor House had showers instead. Downstairs, she put porridge to cook for Si in the slow oven of the range, and bacon for Dessi and herself in the hot. The postman had been, and she was grateful he bothered to deliver today. He usually accumulated the post until it was worth making a delivery: that meant more than ten, so letters arrived late and out-of-date. There was a card from Perdita, more from friends, and also a letter from Jan Morrow.

They hadn't got too far in their world tour, having decided to winter over in the fleshpots of Vienna. Philip had taken to spending his mornings in the coffee houses and his afternoons in the cake shops, eating truffle cake and *sachertorte* and putting on too much weight. He's even insisted on going to a Mozart concert, so Brigid could see they were well into culture. Culture was all very well, but it was bitingly cold, and there wasn't much sun so they'd probably head south to Egypt and do their Pharaohs. Just so long as no one expected her to get up on a camel. Now, would that be all right with Brigid? If it wasn't, would she put the cats in a cattery and let Philip know who to pay? Jan thought perhaps they'd be home for the summer.

It had been a peaceful few weeks since Christmas. Si made himself scarce, spending time in Leeds with friends. Brigid was pleased when he came back, moving slowly through the house, anchoring it down with his tranquillity, making her smile, joking about his parents. At first he ate only raw food to preserve his etheric energy. As the snow persisted, Si decided his etheric energy levels were fine after all, and had some soup and a baked potato. After that he ate everything she cooked with flattering enthusiasm. She began to feel calm herself, more at ease in the cold rooms.

Brigid looked at the snow outside the window and had a childish desire to run in it, to see her spoiling footprints across its pure perfection, to show there was life in this unreal landscape. However, she walked down the garden path without disturbing the wonder of the grass, enjoying the strange shapes of the shrouded shrubs at the end. Under the holly tree snowdrops nestled in igloos of snow mounded over the tent of their leaves. They were less white against the snow, more a greeny cream. They were so simple with their three outer petals, the smaller green-edged ones within, protecting the yellow stamens inside. Brigid had never looked closely at a snowdrop before, and found its stamens curiously optimistic. She bent down to pick a few. They'd look so fresh on the kitchen table. They'd have looked wonderful in the Hebron glass vase if she'd brought it with her.

'Snowdrops should stay in the garden.'

Aeneas was looking down at her, half smiling. Beside him, the Sheltie stood on her toes and tried to tune in her ears to the bleating of the lambs, memory in her genes. It was the first time Brigid had seen Aeneas since the funeral.

Hilly's last rites had been spoilt because the vicar made derogatory remarks about witchcraft, but kindly indicated he was sure God would find it in his heart to forgive Hilly. On leaving the graveyard Aeneas nodded curtly to Cedric and left the outstretched hand unshaken. Bessie told everyone how the vicar had tried to visit Aeneas more than once, but his knock was never answered.

'Sorry,' said Brigid, pulling away from the snowdrops.

Another thing she didn't know. To cover her embarrassment she bent down to the Sheltie. 'Hello Puddle.'

'She's Alys now. I've always called her that . . . Hilly . . . well. I've brought you a birthday present. I hope you don't mind.'

'How do you know it's my birthday?' She looked up from stroking the dog. Aeneas looked different again. His shoulders were no longer bent. He wore no tie, and his shirt hadn't been ironed. Though untidier than ever, he looked more himself, almost relaxed.

'I guessed by your name. This is Brigid's day. Now you want the snowdrops, I'm certain. They're her flowers.' His eyebrows shot up, quizzical, wondering if he'd guessed right. He'd taken a risk, left himself open, vulnerable.

'You're right. I wanted to touch them. Feel their cold. They're so pure. That's what I want now, what's uncomplicated and good.'

'The present is actually from Hilly. She requested it.' He took a couple of steps back and picked up something he'd left on the path. It was a small tree with a root ball of soil encased in a freezer bag.

'It's a Rowan-tree. You're to plant it near to the house.'

'It's not my garden.'

'She wanted it to be while *you're* living here.'

'Why?'

Aeneas shrugged his shoulders and avoided the question. 'It has red berries in the autumn. Would you like me to plant it?'

Hilly'd apologized when she lay in her chair the last time they'd met. Brigid hadn't understood that either. Hilly was confused, but she certainly had something on her mind. 'What about in that corner? I shall see it from the kitchen.' Brigid fetched him a spade. 'It can't be the right time to plant anything,' she said.

'It'll survive,' said Aeneas. 'Hilly will see to that.' He managed to crumble the hard soil beneath the snow with a spade and settled the tree into the earth. He was a mobile man, levering the spade easily.

'I've been tidying out,' he said glancing at her as he spread out the roots. They were resilient and jumped back into their tight ball. 'Trying to shake off winter.' He reminded her of a spring lamb trying to find its legs when he spoke. He was less certain, more secure when silent. 'I'm going through all the drawers. There are things I don't need. Like this. I thought you might like to have it. It will help you understand where you are.' He stood up and stuck the spade in the ground. He rifled through the deep pocket of his waxed jacket and handed her what seemed to be mainly crumpled Christmas wrapping paper. He'd tried to make the present more personal by tying a sprig of myrtle on the top.

Brigid sat on a bench, and unwrapped the present on her knee, in case it was something very tiny she might lose. It was a bronze brooch of Celtic design, about an inch wide. The rings of metal entwined in perpetual circles, never finishing, always moving into a new pattern. Caught within the strands were three tiny fish.

'It's beautiful. Did it belong to Hilly?'

'It belonged to my mother. I never got round to passing it on. It's not living while it sits in a drawer. If you wear it, it'll come alive. Do you understand?'

The sun was already out, and the air had an alpine feel to it, that purity that touches the soul. She smiled up at him. 'Yes. It will be loved.'

'I thought it might help you make out where you are among the Celtic people. The brooch symbolizes renewal. Nothing ends, you see. One circle leads to another.'

'I'm learning.' She pinned the brooch onto the collar of her anorak.

'Or remembering. The Celtic mind doesn't learn. It remembers.'

She was grateful Aeneas could see it wasn't jewellery she wanted, but herself.

'Also to thank you for being kind to Hilly even . . . even if she was difficult.'

'Would you like some breakfast?'

'Could we have it out here?'

'Bacon butties?'

Serves Dessi right, he never gets up at a reasonable time, she thought, as she took their breakfast out of the pan, and put it between slices of toast for Aeneas and herself.

Brigid took the sandwiches and some coffee on a tray to where Aeneas was sitting. He'd found another seat, with a tree stump beside it that would do for a table. She hesitated for a moment. He looked different. She could see him in profile as he looked at the hills. He was no longer blanked out. He looked much younger.

'I heard from the Morrows this morning. They're delaying their return. Philip fell in love with Vienna.'

'Will you stay?'

'I'm not ready to go back yet.'

'We're very down to earth up here. That can help.'

Aeneas was a comforting man. He must have been a kind teacher, a caring one. He saw her unhappiness and tried to help her. She wanted to respond to his kindness, comfort him in return. 'You and Hilly . . .'

'Me and Hilly?'

'I expect you miss her dreadfully.'

Brigid couldn't say exactly what changed. Aeneas finished his sandwich, but he was like the first day they met, remote, away from her in his head. He said, 'I'm just being my dull old self.' He took refuge in a joke, giving himself another layer.

Brigid bit her lip. The moment before, so full of kindness, was gone, and Aeneas was his shuttered self again. Brigid stood up, elegant in her olive leggings and the masculine anorak emphasizing her delicacy. Her hair had lost its stylish definition, but hung in a softer bob. 'The boys will need feeding.' She spotted the sprig of myrtle that had fallen to the ground. She squatted down, supply and easily, to retrieve the stem. She sniffed the fragrance of the blue-green pointed leaves and looked up. Aeneas stood above her with a fleeting bitter apology of a smile. 'Got to walk Alys,' he said turning round. 'Thank you for breakfast.' He nodded and strode towards the car.

'Thank you for the brooch,' she called.

Brigid stood up, and watched him. She'd been stupid, she'd been too inquisitive.

Perhaps he loved Hilly. Though she wasn't a lovable woman. Because she was so vulnerable Brigid wanted to reach out to Aeneas. She wanted the warmth of comforting someone. But he was not hers to reach out toward.

As she walked back to the kitchen door, she passed the newly planted Rowan-tree. She stretched out her hand and touched its leaves. Why did Hilly want her to have it? Something made her pause and she was overcome by a sensation of ease. Although Brigid knew nothing of the Celtic spring, she felt the stirring in the cold earth of a small green shoot called Truth.

She knew that on this her birthday she'd be remembering the best parts of her life with Rupert. Their closeness, created because they did so much together, shared so many creative moments, would comfort her. It was as if they'd always swum in a warm calm sea, and there'd never been a tide to swim against. With a shock she wondered if it were Rupert she really thought about, or their creation of a perfect civility and calm.

Si said, 'That's a new tree.'

'We can take it up before your parents come back,' Brigid said.

'It'll be good for them,' he said. 'It's a Rowan.'

'A bequest from Hilly.'

'Rowan's for protection. Hilly was a witch.'

'Why should she want to protect me?'

'Some spell?'

'Si, what is willow for? She told me to take it into the house at Christmas.'

'Willow is an underworld tree, a tree of the dark aspect of the goddess. Its sign is used to contact the dark gods. The willow is a tree of suffering. Remember Ophelia.'

The snow lingered for a long time. However, by the end of February it felt as if spring were coming. A hedge of forsythia beyond the vegetables was glowing like Spanish gold in the twilight. There was bergenia in the hedge bottom, and daffodils under the wall. Si washed his sap green robe, and hung it on the line to dry in the wind. It billowed like a huge verdant sail over the grass.

Having done all she could in the house, Brigid spent time in the garden, digging the damp dark earth, clearing the weeds from the previous year, making it wholesome and ready for its fertility. She took suggestions from Si. A curved bed here, a shifted shrub there. Dessi tried to help but he left weeds lying around on top of the soil. She loved the smell of it, warm and damp, felt the vibration of its sleeping life, sensed the richness that could come. Eventually, all the vegetable garden was prepared, ready for its role in life. She sat cross-legged on the grass beside it. She was tired but she suddenly felt young, almost as she had before she met Rupert. She wasn't surprised that Aeneas didn't come round to see her again. He'd come as a friend, and left as Hilly's husband.

Later that week, Brigid woke in the night, and lay listening to the sounds of the night. She wasn't certain what had woken her. It wasn't the sheep because lambing was finished and the ewes were calm, except when one strayed. She thought she could hear something in the garden below her window. Reluctantly, she got out of bed and looked through the window.

Below her Si sat on the lawn, looking up at the pearly white of the moon. He was completely starkers. His clothes lay beside him in a neat folded pile. 'You'll get worse than piles,' said Brigid. She put on her dressing-gown and, being cold, her anorak over that. She went to the kitchen and put the kettle on the range.

The kitchen curtains were open, and the light stretched out onto the garden. Si turned his head. He stood up. Brigid closed her eyes. When he came through the door he was tucking his shirt into his trousers, Brigid was glad to see.

'Not ever so clever.' She blamed him for waking her up in the first place.

'I was moon bathing. It's amazing more people don't do it. You need to touch both the sun and the moon to strike a balance.'

'It's lunatic,' said Brigid pouring two mugs of tea, 'to sit naked out there in February.'

'Sky-clad. A more attractive term for the state of nature. I need toast.' Si put bread on the hot plate. 'Moon bathing sky-clad makes you hungry.' He stood in front of the range, and began to steam. His clothes had soaked up damp from the grass.

'What *is* all this about?'

'It goes back a long way.'

Brigid sat down at the table, and pointed to the chair opposite. 'Begin at the beginning,' she said, mocking him. 'Time is a more cosmic element than space.'

'It was when I went away to school. I hated it. I mean, *really* hated it. I thought it was me, you know, thought I really was inferior. I got teased. They said I was thick. Bullied really, because I wasn't good at games, or at work, and I wasn't funny. I wasn't good looking. Four essentials. You've got to be one of them to survive. I wasn't any of them. I was small too. I got to be the punch bag. Squatty, they called me.

'It was worse when people knew we'd got a big house. Money. Lots of it. Money complex. Not enough like Dessi, and you're out. Too much was worse. It had to *be* there, but in short supply. Tricky thing to get just right. Mine was the sort of minor public school parents chose because it was the cheapest, and they'd rather have a crap public school than a decent free state Grammar. *I* was there because it was the only school that would take me. It was a lousy school. Three of the staff up on sex charges in two years. God, I wasn't even attractive enough for that.

'Dad gave a cup for public spirit. It could be won by anyone without any talent at all. I didn't win that either. It was the biggest cup the school ever had. It was a laughing stock. They called it the *pubic* spirit.' Si bit noisily into his toast. Brigid passed him a plate and some butter. He spread the toast by drawing the face of it over the surface of the yellow slab. Crumbs fastened on to the pristine surface. He pushed the plate out of reach. Brigid winced.

'Then,' said Si, 'I learned to meditate. Things got different. I stopped being frightened of them. I saw them as they were. Pretty feeble people. I saw their weakness and I could see their pain. I realized I could help them. I could make guys feel good. Dessi was the biggest twit of all, so I helped him the most. Not a twit in the sense of being stupid. He was a scholarship boy, the only one. The others didn't like scholarship boys, they weren't up to it on the financial scale. He hadn't got the pocket money and his parents took him to Blackpool for his holidays. You had to be just like the others, shabby but arrogant. He was a twit in that he couldn't cope with them any better than I could.

'Then I stood back. I didn't compete with their little egos. I gave people space to grow. It helped Dessi. He stopped working. Began to get more popular, but he got into smoking. The weed, that is. There was a lot around. He hadn't got the money, so he did essays for other boys instead. It all came out when some really on the ball teacher noticed two-thirds of the class wrote that Henry the Eighth married Lady Jane Grey. Because Dessi told the truth instead of lying through his teeth, he got expelled. He was an example, and they wouldn't have to teach him for free anymore.

'We kept up. Except he didn't. He went down. He kept writing to let me know his latest scrape. Think he hoped I'd bale him out. I often did. He never did get his education.'

'There's a gleam in Dessi,' said Brigid, 'if he weren't so slow. Surprises me with what he comes out with. So you solved your problem?'

'I began to realize I'm a . . . a conduit, if you like. Yes, a conduit for the godhead.' Si shut his eyes, and leaned back in the chair. He gave a long, slow sigh, as if he'd shed a weight from his shoulders.

'A sort of a drain?' Brigid suggested, picking individual crumbs off the surface of the butter.

'Very droll.'

'Sorry. No, I *am* sorry. Just vocabulary. First impression. The Romans called their *drains* conduits.'

'Stop using that word.'

'Yes, I'm sorry. Conduit. Definitely conduit. Not in the plumbing sense at all.'

'I'm not just *getting along* any more. I had power. For the first time I was someone. Then came the healing. If I put spit on a rugby gash it'd heal quicker.'

'Dog lick does that too.' Brigid poured more tea.

'Some dogs are very *spiritual.*'

'There are enzymes in saliva that deal with bacteria.'

Si didn't want to know. 'Now let's talk about you,' he said. 'You haven't come back to me with your problem.'

'I'm not the confiding type,' said Brigid. 'Anyway, I'm feeling better now.'

'I know,' said Si nodding. 'I know.'

'So I'm OK, thank you.'

'But not completely OK, are you? You can't mourn.

That's it, isn't it? You can't mourn Rupert.'

'No.' Brigid found Si's perception alarming.

'No. Why's that? I can feel the pain now.'

Brigid stared at her cup. The tea was from the box of Jan's cheap bags. She'd been too tired to notice which ones she was taking. There was an orange tide mark. Strange how much more vulnerable one is in the small hours, much more afraid of any problem. She was tempted to tell Si what happened at the funeral. After all, he'd confided in her. She pushed her tea mug round the table in a gesture of reluctance. Si would come out with a fatuous platitude.

'I feel resistance,' he said. 'You're not ready yet, are you? Some day, you'll tell me or someone else. Let's do more toast. You want some?'

'I think I might.' The threat of Si's analysis subsided and Brigid felt better for that. She watched him toast the bread, inspecting it too often and slowing up the process. Outside it was dark but the kitchen seemed friendly. She'd bought a new red-check cloth for the table to replace the burned one.

The range clicked as the heat within it reaffirmed itself. She felt warm and considerably comforted. She breathed in, then let the air escape at its own speed. Si watched the last phase of the toast. She was suddenly hungry.

A year ago she wouldn't have dreamed of drinking tea in the middle of the night with a New Age messiah. Even less that she'd feel comfortable with him. She fingered the bronze brooch Aeneas gave her, which was still pinned to the collar of her anorak. She felt the continuity within it, she took comfort in the endlessness of it.

Si handed her a piece of toast. There was no knife

with the butter. To get one out of the knife drawer meant walking across the kitchen. Slowly and deliberately, Brigid dragged the toast across the surface of the butter, acquiring a thick golden layer of it, along with crumbs deposited by Si's earlier piece. She crammed it into her mouth, half the slice in one go. 'Umm,' she said, and closed her eyes to feel more urgently the consolation of the butter melting on her tongue.

Brigid stared at the surface of the slab of butter, scarred and speckled with brown crumbs. She wiped a dribble of melted butter off the corner of her mouth. Was she getting like her mother, regressing to a messy slut? She was not. She was getting more like Aunt Roo. Untrammelled. Like Celtic wild and wonderful Aunt Roo.

The cat flap clattered and Tara poured herself through the small aperture. She deposited the half-eaten body of a vole at Si's feet, and went back outside. Si stared at the bones and entrails arranged in a pattern beside his left shoe. 'I must read the portents,' and he sat admiring the bloody mess, this sign of encouragement from his totem beast, this sign from Tara that he only need interpret.

'You can clear that up,' said Brigid. 'I'm going to bed.' She picked up the other half of her toast and went upstairs, crunching quite noisily.

Vernal Equinox

Christianity came to Britain in two ways. It came first with the wandering prophets and monks as they made their way through Europe from the Middle East. It was Patrick who brought the word to Ireland, and then on to Iona. It was Aiden who took the word from the west coast to the east, from Iona to Lindisfarne. Cuthbert succeeded him there at the monastery. The island of Lindisfarne was a particularly sacred place in Celtic Christianity, and apart from its innate beauty, was celebrated for its association with the revered St Cuthbert. However, he found even this place too worldly, and spent most of his time on the Farne islands. These Celts wove Christianity into their pagan faith, intermingling it with nature. They were Christians in their faith, but pagans in their hearts, living close to the earth and its natural forces. Then came Augustine, Paulinus and Wilfred and their ilk, bringing the Roman version of Christianity, which had developed hierarchies and priests, pomp and ceremony and the subordination of women. There was a showdown at the synod of Whitby in 664 AD, hosted incidentally by a woman, Hilda. Roman-orientated Wilfred eventually became Archbishop of York. Ironically, it was not these fundamental differences that split Christianity at the time, but two smaller issues of the correct procedure for calculating Easter, and how monks should wear their hair.

Although he accepted the ruling of Rome at the Synod of Whitby, Cutherbert was a man more concerned with spirituality than with dogma, and spent the most part of his life in meditation and solitude. His followers so revered him that when he died the monks carried his body with them for forty years until they found a safe resting place for it in Durham Cathedral.

The Celtic Way, A.B.W.

Si eventually interpreted his sign from Tara, his totem beast, his link with the godhead. The message in the entrails was that he should take action. He spent hours contemplating what that should be. He never doubted Tara's profoundly spiritual role, but thought the cat should have been more specific. Tara stared at him, her green eyes full of scorn for his leaden mind. Brigid spotted his predicament and encouraged contact by insisting he took over the feline catering. Since Tara wasn't eating out of tins, this helped Brigid, but was no advantage whatever to Si.

'Do you think I'll ever have a totem beast?' Dessi asked.

'No.'

'I don't think so either.'

Early on a Tuesday morning in mid-March, Si concluded the action must involve his following. Si must reassemble his flock. The solstice bonfire had been a success, and who knows where it might have led had it not been for the cardboard camel. When better for an assembly than on the Vernal equinox, which was about to come up? The locals thought March the twenty-first was the first day of spring, but spring had begun in February. It was instead the moment when the time of light balanced exactly the time of dark. It was the focal point of the spring season. 'Let's have a barbie, Dessi. On the beach at Beadnell.' That was the nearest bit of coast. 'Lots of water to epitomize the fluidity of the New Age.'

Si designed a poster with figures robed in sap green dispensing veggiburgers from a stone altar. *A New Age Flowering*, said the letters in an arch at the top, and at the bottom it read, *Love it.* At the top was a lemon cloud. 'The Higher Intelligence,' explained Si, 'and then I realized you can't draw that so I tried to wash it away. Rather a good effect, yeah?'

'You said there *wasn't* a higher intelligence. Just a universal soul,' said Dessi.

'I told you wrong.'

'There can't be both,' said Dessi. 'It'd be like having Tesco and Asda in the same building.'

'Pin it on Bessie's door,' said Si, 'and stop quibbling.'

'Kebabs would be tasty,' said Bessie. 'Shall I get some lamb in?'

Si grasped her warmly by the shoulders. 'Not meat, darlin',' he said, 'but could you locate some tofu?'

'Never come across tofu.' Bessie was doubtful. 'Chick pea patties I might unearth.'

The vicar, who always came in for his *Radio Times* about now read the new notice on the door. He stormed into the shop. 'What profane lark might this be then?'

'Not profane, Cedric. Profoundly spiritual. You can come if you don't bring an amplifier.'

'I shall be keeping my beadies on you.'

'Well, darlin', you've nothing to lose but your fundamentals.'

'Don't "darling" me, young man. What are you? A sodding poufter or something?'

'As a matter of fact, no. I'm dangerously hetero. It's

amazing how homophobic Christians are in a religion dominated by single men.'

'Well, I hope we'll have none of the other going on either.'

'You have a problem, Cedric. Do you need to share it with me? Remember, I'm always here for you. Basically, you're obsessed by sex, aren't you? Admit it.' Si smiled. 'Darlin'.'

Come the morning of the gathering, the thought of action made Si torpid. He lay in bed and Brigid fed the cats herself. Dessi was in his usual black and yellow striped sweater, washing it overnight and drying it on the range. With each wash it got smaller. He patrolled the kitchen like a demented wasp, his auburn curls bouncing round his head like lottery balls out on the town. He rattled through the saucepan cupboard, trying to decide what he needed. 'We'll have to go shopping,' he said.

'Don't touch my new wok,' Brigid threatened. 'It's to add variety to vegetarian cuisine.'

The day was fresh, with that brightness that promises heat later on, and would produce haze to make the hills look unreal and mystical. There were daffodils out in the garden and the forsythia was beginning to replace the winter jasmine and glow bright yellow in the hedges. She was surprised when Aeneas appeared at the front door. He looked apprehensive.

'Aeneas. Hello?'

'In case you go away,' Aeneas said, 'I want you to remember a certain place as it is today. We should go there for a picnic.' The words came out quickly, as if well rehearsed. He looked down at the table while he waited for an answer.

'I'm not thinking of leaving at the moment,' said Brigid, 'but can I still come?'

'You will?'

'Wasn't I supposed to say yes?'

'I thought you might be busy.'

'Picnic? I've got some cold chicken.'

'The picnic's done,' said Aeneas. 'In the car. I picked it up on the way.'

Brigid went upstairs and shouted outside Si's door. 'I'm off for the day. See you this evening.'

'What about our breakfast? And lunch?' He sounded half asleep, but concerned.

'The world is a wonderful place,' Brigid said. 'It will provide. Don't bother about trivialities.'

'Shit,' said Si. 'Give Dessi a call, will you. Tell the lazy bum to get some breakfast.'

Aeneas drove slowly along the lanes, and even on reaching the A1, continued as if the road were still narrow and winding. Eventually he took a turn right, and made towards the coast. 'No point in getting there before eleven.'

'We're going to Lindisfarne,' Brigid realized. 'I don't know why I've not been before.'

'You were waiting for me to take you,' said Aeneas, smiling at her.

Brigid knew that was a joke, yet there was something disconcertingly serious in everything he said. It was as if he believed she'd go to the island for the first time with him. Even so, the words weren't personal. Aloofness still lurked.

Brigid looked at him without turning her head too much, pretending to look at the view to the right. His eyes dominated his face. They were calm, yet vulnerable, wise and humorous. A capacity for compassion was evident within them, yet he would allow no-one to look within, and see what he thought. He didn't exert his compassion. He was wary.

They crossed the causeway to the island of Lindisfarne at eleven, after watching the road emerge from the sea like a recumbent stone goddess. As they drove across, the mudflats on either side shone like beaten pewter in the sun. Grasses and reeds grew out of the water, and wading whimbrels and redshanks dipped and drilled into the mud.

They left the causeway and Aeneas looked back. 'Holy Island,' he said, 'isn't an island any more.'

From the car park she could see the priory glowing in the sun to the south, high on its rock, its roofless arches warm with centuries of goodness. Aeneas took a rucksack out of the boot, and pointed in the opposite direction. 'We're going to a little bay at Snipe Point,' he said. 'Over the dunes, and away from all this.'

'Not the priory?'

'No. All that remains are what was built long after Cuthbert lived here. That's not what Lindisfarne's about.'

They walked out of the village in the opposite direction to all the other visitors, and along a track that moved first between fields and then gave way to moorland. The track became silty. Ahead of them sand dunes rose up, too high to be able to see the sea beyond. Eventually the track disappeared. They walked past a hunched hawthorn bush and had to avoid stepping on tiny helleborines like white flat buttercups. They climbed through the dunes, and at the top, the land fell away to a protected sandy bay, with mud flats stretching out as the tide receded.

'Snipe bay,' said Aeneas with a shy air of triumph.

He unpacked the rucksack. Out came two bottles of beer, which he put into the sea to cool, screwing the bottles into the sand. 'Leek pasties,' he said. 'Bessie made them specially for you. She's known for her pasties. Sort of thing Harrods would stock if they knew where to find them.' He was mocking her.

'Sophisticated leek pasties,' she said, mocking him back, and immediately wishing she hadn't in case he thought she was making fun of the simple pleasure of a picnic.

'Holy Island,' said Brigid. 'It still feels holy to me, here. It's the peace. It's as if nothing could ever jar.'

'Islands are always holy places. They're apart from the material, from the politic. They're cleansed by the water which surrounds them. To reach them you must make a journey. The Celts believed the other world overlaid this, and in some places you could cross between the two. An island was such a place. This will be an island again in a few hours. In the Celtic mind, the ninth wave was the boundary of the land. At high tide, Lindisfarne would be its own place.'

Aeneas looked at her as he spoke, but he'd focused his mind on his argument, not on her face. He moved his hands, drawing with them, raised and lowered his voice for emphasis. Brigid knew he must have been a persuasive teacher.

'Did you always want to teach?'

'I wanted to learn first, I suppose. My parents didn't understand what university was. They didn't know anyone who'd been there. They thought I should work on the land.'

'I supposed you were from an academic family. Your name, I suppose.'

'Right. Yes. Latin. I think I was named after the schoolmaster's cat. Mother thought the name was from the Bible. She must have fancied Mr Collier, looking back.'

'At least he inspired you?'

'He was a generous man. He taught us all to swim. All his boys. We used to go into the sea with our waterwings. Amazingly buoyant. We'd have drowned without them. Him teaching seven or eight of us at once.'

'They have arm bands now,' said Brigid, remembering hours and hours in chlorinated swimming baths with Kit and Perdita as they splashed and bobbed and spluttered their way across.

'I'm glad I had waterwings,' said Aeneas. 'The word, with the *w*'s fits better. *B*'s and *d*'s have no affinity with their purpose. Too rigid. No fluidity. We'd never have had arm bands in the sea with Mr Collier.'

'Are your parents still alive?'

'No. They were old when they had me.'

'They'd be proud of you.'

'I wasn't proud. I was a real country loaf. And the women. They *terrified* me. They could *dance*. They sang bits from *Don Giovanni* and *Cliff Richard*. No-one ate *tea*. If they did, it was only cake. Nothing with a knife and fork. They spent a lot of money on clothes. Without a second thought. I was so ignorant.'

'You did make some friends?'

'General friends. Not special. There was Roni Carver. She had *flying* lessons. She was as tall as me and she wore a hat, a large droopy one made of faded cotton. Black. No-one else wore a hat. She smoked Turkish cigarettes. They don't smell horrible, you know. Very sweet. I really wanted to go out with her.

'That's why I decided to teach. Help people not to be like me.'

'So you came back here.'

'I didn't plan to. I thought I'd be headmaster one day of a big school in the south. I met Hilly. She was easy to talk to.' He sounded resigned. 'She was . . . undemanding.'

'And she was pretty.'

'Yes.'

'She cast a spell on you.' Brigid intended this as a tribute to the younger Hilly, to show Aeneas she knew his wife hadn't always been unattractive. Brigid imagined Hilly as she might have been, slim with her thick mouth and big breasts. Aeneas, intimidated by the Durham students, was trapped by nature.

'Yes. She cast a spell all right. It was guilt. A child not coming.'

'Poor Hilly.'

'She blamed me. But it was her. I got the results from the hospital first. I never told her. I was all she had. I became her child. I wanted children. Proper children.'

'What was Hilly doing in the spinney, last Christmas?'

'Hilly thought she was a witch. She communed. That sort of thing. She went in for a lot of communing when she wanted a child.' He shrugged, deliberately vague.

'She was casting a spell that night.'

'You think?' Aeneas shifted his position to stare out across the sea.

'I'm not really sure.'

'Nothing's happened to you has it?'

'I didn't say she cast a spell on *me*.'

'Of course not.' Aeneas looked up at the sky.

'Hilly didn't like me.'

'She thought you were attractive. Too elegant for

round here is what she said.'

'Why did she send the Rowan-tree, Aeneas?'

He shrugged. 'I suppose she felt her negative thoughts might harm you. I don't know.'

'She was praying to the moon.'

'She drew down the moon for extra strength. She thought . . . she thought . . . you were like the girls at Durham. She tried to harm you. I don't know. I tried to stop her. She wasn't one to be restrained. She wanted you to pick willow. Supposed to be bad luck. Then there was the wine at Christmas. I didn't know about that till later.'

'What was the wine supposed to do?'

'Create havoc, I think. But when she was dying, she thought better of it. She sent the Rowan-tree.'

'It doesn't matter. Nothing has happened.'

Brigid enjoyed being with Aeneas. He wasn't the dull man she'd first seen. He was more worldly, but not artificial or sophisticated. Worldly and naïve at the same time.

She sat back with the sun warm on her face, she felt the coarseness of the sand and grass beneath her, listened to the cry of the gulls wheeling above her head and the ceaseless lapping of the water. The breeze pulled at her sweater, and she felt as if she were a part of this landscape, a part of the island. And the island was part of the whole of life. There was a totality to it. Life with Rupert had been so exclusive of the world, almost superficial, a fabrication of material perfections. Today, that past life seemed almost like a shell, a beautiful and hollow shell. She needed to find the kernel, the heart within. She had to discover the essence of herself.

* * *

After the picnic they walked back along the coast. Aeneas helped her over some slippery rocks. He took her hand, and she jumped down beside him. For a moment, they stood face to face, looking at each other.

Abruptly, Aeneas let go of her hand and said, 'We must get back or the causeway will be under water.' He walked on. Brigid knew that wasn't true. There was plenty of time before the tide would engulf the road again.

She caught him up and said, 'I've enjoyed today. Loved it.' She meant to add that he shouldn't feel she expected anything of him because he'd invited her here.

'Have you *really*?'

'Really.'

'One day I'll take you to another island. Inner Farne. It's too crowded at the moment, full of visitors gawping at the wildlife.' He stood looking down at her with his teasing smile, which he seemed to find so hard to display. 'Perhaps in a year and a day,' he said.

They walked at a leisurely pace, exploring the flowers and grasses, talking about when he'd been a teacher. Brigid was about to ask him about the book Hilly said he was writing.

'I don't know anything about you,' he said. 'Only what I see.' He raised one quizzical eyebrow.

She didn't know what to say. Her life would sound trivial if she tried to put it into words. She opened her handbag, slung round her shoulders like a satchel. 'I've got a photo,' she said, 'of when I was younger.' It was a picture taken of Brigid with Rupert at a dinner. She was wearing a teal green silk dress, of a willowy cut and Rolando had done a particularly good job on her hair. Rupert, in his dinner jacket, was smiling down at her protectively. She carried it with her because it was a good photo of Rupert. In front of them on the table was a clutter of glasses and flowers.

Brigid regretted showing it the minute she handed it over. It was a life so far away from how she lived now, it seemed nothing to do with her.

'The girls at Durham were like that.' Aeneas spoke in a flat voice. The animation had gone. 'You look very happy.'

'I thought I was,' she said, trying to repair the damage. She wanted to tell him about . . . and decided against it. They walked faster now, the ease marred, the spell of the island broken.

'It's been lovely,' said Brigid.

'Yes,' said Aeneas, and she still couldn't tell what he was thinking.

They crossed the causeway on the incoming tide. In places the water lapped at the tyres, and Aeneas drove faster as if the tide could overtake them and cut them off. He drove home down the coast. They stopped to look over Bamburgh castle, then had a beer and some sandwiches in a bar overlooking the sea. When they were nearly home, he said, 'Shall we see what mad Si is up to?'

It was dusk when they got to Beadnell Bay. There was the familiar lemon van. A narrow sandy path led to the beach, where a small fire, with a spit built above it, dived and darted in the wind. Dessi was frying vegetables in Brigid's new wok. He'd never get it clean again. 'You should get a wok,' she said to Aeneas. 'It's a quick way of cooking.'

'I'm not a wok type,' he said. 'I'm anchored to these shores.'

Si stood by the sea, apparently paddling.

Aeneas and Brigid went over to Dessi, suddenly feeling hungry.

'Is Si paddling?' Aeneas asked. It seemed unlikely.

'Si wouldn't paddle. It's naff. He might swim. Naked. Not paddle. He's contemplating the deep.'

'From the shallows,' said Aeneas.

Si came back from the sea edge, and saw them. 'Come and eat,' he called and broke off a large chunk of bread from the loaf he was holding. 'What have you two been up to?' He sounded suspicious, with a hint of conspiracy.

Brigid wondered whether it was the glow of the fire that made Aeneas look as if he were blushing, or if he really was. She was pleased and said, 'We've been to Lindisfarne.'

'Oh, that,' said Si. 'Monks and seagulls.'

'They're coming,' said Dessi. 'There's Bessie, and the fat woman from the last house. Hell. We've got bloody Cedric.' There were two youths who held cigarettes between thumb and forefinger, and a girl in a leather skirt eleven inches deep. *They* soon disappeared into the dunes. There was the youth of Beadnell out for a freebie, and a couple of fishermen on their way home.

'Hail,' said Si. He wore his sap green robe. When he waved his arms, the spare cloth tended to flap around the wrists. Instead, he held his arms up, the sleeves slipping away down his wrists and his hands extended in a willowy blessing. Cedric ducked, wishing to avoid an Aquarian benediction.

'There's no meat,' said Bessie, looking in the wok. 'You've only got vegetables.'

'Fresh,' said Dessi. He stopped himself explaining they'd got them from Berwick that morning because

Bessie's cabbages were distinctly shrivelled and her parsnips large and woody.

'Hello Aeneas,' said Bessie. She didn't notice Brigid. 'Got a nice bit of ham hock on the simmer at home.' She giggled.

'Never been one for ham hock,' said Aeneas.

Si produced a bunch of daffodils from behind a rock, began to strew them in a circle around himself on the sand. 'For the goddess.'

'For the *what*?' Dessi said. '*Si*?' Dessi shook his head. 'It was all energy. No god on a cloud thing. Where did *she* come from?'

'As you go deeper,' said Si clasping Dessi by the shoulders, 'things emerge. They're made known to me.'

'This I suspected,' said Cedric, coming forward, dressed casually for the barbecue in olive cord trousers and a rose-coloured cabled thick knit that had shrunk and fitted snugly round the curves of his stomach and bottom. He resembled an outraged chaffinch. 'Pagan rites again. When I saw the notice on Bessie's door, I knew what would go on.'

'If I were you, I'd dissociate myself double quick,' said Si, 'because I'm now going to bury an egg in each quarter of the flower circle, to guarantee fertility of this place. The goddess is awake.'

'Have some corn on the cob, Vicar,' said Dessi, eager to keep Si out of trouble.

'I can't sully myself with this nonsense,' said Cedric, and stood to one side, looking huffy. 'The man's a heathen.'

Si's brown eyes were especially bright. 'I won't embarrass you Cedric, I'll leave the rites until you've gone. You're free to eat. I haven't blessed the wok yet so there's nothing spiritual there to upset your stomach.' He nodded and walked away, smiling in a way that didn't bode well for Cedric. Besides, proper followers were slow to show up. There was a disappointing absence. He was in no hurry.

'Well . . .' Cedric was enticed but didn't recognize it as temptation. He chose the largest piece of corn on the cob, dipped it in the bowl of butter and champed into the honeyed kernels.

'How are you settling, Brigid? I keep hoping you'll visit us on a Sunday. Sung Eucharist first in every month, matins on the last. Evensong whenever we can fit it in.'

'I never went at home,' said Brigid, 'except socially. I don't do that anymore.'

'Socially is better than nothing,' said Cedric. 'Something might rub off.'

Brigid tried to avoid watching the butter dripping down his thick knit. Aeneas handed him some bread to mop it up, more to register disgust than be helpful.

'Very kind, Aeneas. I was hoping, now that Hilly's gone . . .' Cedric began, when only a faint tawny stain remained. 'You might return to the fold.'

'Now Hilly is gone?'

'The influence, you know. All that widdershins business. Should I exorcize the cottage?'

Aeneas stared at Cedric.

'Difficult woman. Leave it a while, shall we? Then try matins. Nothing like a nice matins. No shifting out of your pew.' Cedric looked optimistically for some response. 'Try to climb back on the raft, old chap. You'll find the parish very understanding.' Cedric shrugged his shoulders and took another cob of corn.

'Where is everyone?' Dessi asked. 'We thought

everyone would come after the bonfire.'

'Quiz night at the Woolpack,' said Bessie. 'With a happy hour at the start.'

'*We* could go to that,' said Aeneas, perking up.

'Look,' said Dessi suddenly. 'Look over there. On the sea.'

It was dark now, and a faint moon lit the water. The waves were quite strong, the water wasn't sleeping. Over to the right, twenty or so yards from the shore stood a man on the sea.

He glided like a light moving up with the swell of the wave, towards the shingle, towards the shore. He stretched out his arms, and his robe flowed with the sway of his body as it answered to the rhythms of the sea. He seemed to come nearer, then recede. With one surge he came forward again.

'Si's walking on water,' said Dessi.

Cedric stood open-mouthed as he watched the figure reach the shore. With a realignment of his body, Si's mode changed, and he was earthbound again. He strode back along the beach towards them. Even in the dim light Brigid saw the triumphant smile on his face. He came up, his eyes fixed on Cedric.

'Jesus,' said Bessie, and sat down.

The vicar, with a strangled cry, ran off the beach. He climbed in his car, drove back to the village, unlocked the church and flung himself down in front of the altar, demanding to know of God what was going on.

When Brigid got back to the house she went to the back porch. As she expected, the surf board was gone.

Dessi walked alone along the beach, back to where Si made his landing. He stood for a long time looking down at the water margin, at the water gurgling over the shingle, at the flotsam around the creamy rim of the water. He looked at the large piece of shaped wood beached above the water.

The Vernal equinox marked the turning point of the sun. It marked the turning point of more than one person who moved beneath it that day. Dessi was hurt. He felt as he had when his mother packed him off to boarding school on his scholarship. He had the same sensation in his stomach as when his brains at school had impressed no one. Again, he'd misplaced his trust.

'Why did you have to do that?' Dessi asked Si later.

'You've got to get their attention. The end justifies the means.'

When Dessi came down to breakfast the next morning, he wore a clean white poplin shirt instead of his shrunken wasp sweater. He'd slicked his hair back to reveal his deep forehead. Gone were the boyish bouncy curls. He'd been at them with the scissors.

Beltaine

Beltaine means bright fire. In the Celtic world this festival marked the beginning of summer, around May 1st. May day, until recently, was celebrated in rural areas with May poles and other fetility rites, which was in contradiction to a summer said now to start in June. It was a time when animals were let out of the byres to roam freely on the open pasture, because the climate was mellow. It was a time for coming into strength, and realizing desires. Life was at its most intense with flowers everywhere, birds in full song, and every potential about to be fulfilled.

It was a time of pilgrimage, for the blood stirred in men's veins. The Celts even went to sea rudderless, allowing the currents, tides and winds to take them to a destination known only to the gods. At home, young girls bathed their faces in dew to enhance their maidenhood and to hope for the coming of their life's partner. Moreover, Beltaine was a time for visiting. It was a time for release. The blood stirred in the veins of the poet.

The Celtic Way, A.B. Westlake

Aeneas came round from time to time and he was as remote as he'd been before Hilly died. The friendship Brigid sensed on Holy Island was no longer there. She'd spoiled that by showing him the photo of Rupert and herself. She'd reinforced the image of herself as artificial, the one she'd given originally which was totally alien to him. He was pleasant and courteous, and treated her with some care. Brigid wondered if he only saw her brittle and untouchable in her evening dress, and with Rupert looking so loving beside her. Or was it that he still loved Hilly?

Aeneas *was* changing in other ways. He was rebuilding his life. He walked taller and with more energy. He was outgoing to the rest of the village and they warmed to him, where previously they'd found him aloof, even superior. He joked with people he never used to speak to, his eyes that had once been mocking were now only teasing. It was as if he were getting back his spring, after being reduced to the mundane for so long by Hilly.

Brigid walked by his cottage one morning half meaning to call and see him. Rhododendrons were out in the gardens, alongside bluebells and clematis Montana. Cherry blossom lay snowed into drifts on the paths. She wanted the comfort of talking to a civilized person. Si was comfortable in his being there, but still determined to pry into her past and *heal* her.

Aeneas was sitting among the trees where Hilly once practised her spells. On a small table before him was his typewriter, and beside him, on the grass, a pile of reference books. He was pecking away at the keys with the middle finger of each hand, sometimes tapping faster, occasionally reaching down to pick up a book from beside him on the grass. He wore a check cotton shirt that was a bit thick for the day, but Aeneas wasn't a man to plan his wardrobe. His hair, too long at the back, stuck out above his collar in untidy clumps. He drank from a coffee mug as she watched, clasping it around the middle, ignoring the handle, and putting it back in the grass by his foot without taking his eyes from the paper. He was lost to the world in his work. She wanted to ask about the book he was writing, but he seemed too private, too complete in his world of words to need to share.

Brigid felt she was spying on him, as she had once spied on Hilly. She was an intruder and turned away.

May became June and summer arrived beyond doubt. 'Why haven't you gone south and stopped them building this by-pass?' asked Brigid, coming into the drawing-room with the Hoover.

Si stood by the window which looked out to the side of the house. By pushing his head against the glass, and screwing his eyes round till they hurt he could just look across the front oval of lawn, painted with a light, bright dew, and down the road to the valley.

'That's work for the troops,' he said. 'We've all been there. I'm here for something quite different.'

He watched Tara walk snootily out through the gate. He nodded. 'I got you,' he called through the glass. 'I did what you told me.'

Brigid opened the other heavy sash windows to let in the summer air.

'We must shop,' said Si. 'Get in supplies.'

'Supplies?'

'For the others. They're coming. I've sent out vibrations. Telephoned them as well, just in case. But they said they'd got them. The vibrations. Telepathy is all very well, but it's not a totally reliable form of communication.'

'What others *exactly*?'

'From the wider world. The village is barren ground. They turned me down, remember, for the happy hour and pub quiz. A prophet in his own land and all that.'

'Will they be house guests?' Brigid switched off the Hoover. She hadn't got Si and Dessi's housekeeping arrangements sorted out even after six months. There were sundry contributions when income support benefit turned up, but no fixed housekeeping agreement. Dessi found calculations difficult, and Si was above that sort of thing.

'Unless they need to be outdoors.' Si was reluctant to say yes. 'They may have their vans. The time has come for proper followers, not the brain dead from round here.'

'Highmoor House will become irresistible to even the most enthusiastic campers,' said Brigid, 'because of the bath and the washing machine. Will they be *your* guests or mine?'

'What do you mean?'

'I mean, who's paying for the food?'

'Brigid. Brigid. You're so tied up with trivialities. The world is a wonderful place. It provides for all.'

'Not the view of Bessie. Or Somerfields.'

'A worker should have what he needs. I came to this house, and you welcomed me, so I stayed. Don't withdraw your welcome now, Brigid. Not now that such an important time is come.'

'This *is* your house,' said Brigid coldly. 'Come to think of it, your parents could turn up any time. I think I'll go back to Wimbledon.'

'You can't do that. Your house is being let.'

'Ever heard of friends?'

Si turned round and smiled his wonderful full-faced smile, embracing her with his eyes, pulling her into the warm circle of his confidence. 'They'll all adore you,' he said. 'There's simply no-one like you.' He held up a finger and moved it like a benediction.

In response she wagged her own finger back at him, 'Trivialities resolve themselves. No problem. *Darlin'*,' she added.

'You'll miss the fun.' Si stopped the benediction which he didn't like to see mocked. 'Come on, Brigid, stay. You're magic.'

'As a cook, you mean,' said Brigid. She thought of her carefully created home, and wondered if the tenants were treating it properly. They were on a month by month contract now as the Morrows were so vague about their plans, but they were keen to stay. For a moment she ached to be back there. Harvey and Esther were out of the question because Esther might have come across further variations on the theme of mince. She could only go to Murray and Jennifer. There'd be the questions and the meaningful silences. There'd be the sympathy and manufactured treats. That was even *less* inviting than slaving away for Si's unseen hangers-on.

'OK,' she said. 'You and Dessi can shop. On your own. I'll make the list.'

While Si and Dessi were in Alnwick, Brigid opened up the other bedrooms. They were musty, the staleness steeped into the woodwork. Fresh air off the Cheviots would never prevail in one day. These were the rooms of the Morrow children who'd fled the nest, and Jan had done nothing to update them. There were still posters of Shakin' Stephens and Georgie Fame on the wardrobe doors. There were postcards from Corfu stuck on the mirror. Postcards written at a time when people went to Corfu in the footsteps of Gerald Durrell. Brought out again for the grandchildren was a lamp shaped like a toadstool with a sleeping rabbit family within, and a mobile of Taiwan parasols. It would have been a pleasure to set up the beds with linen or cotton, but she could only find a variety of knitted nylon fitted sheets in a diversity of greens.

The phone rang. 'It's Perdita. I'm coming to see you. That OK?'

'More than OK. When?'

'Not absolutely certain.'

'Never mind. It'll be wonderful to see you,' said Brigid. 'How are you?'

'All right.'

'Not more than all right?'

'See you.'

'How are you getting here?' The line went dead.

Brigid was relieved to get another letter next morning from the Morrows postponing their return yet again. To explain the occupancy of all the bedrooms would be embarrassing. Jan didn't give the impression of being hospitable. They'd reached India, and Philip was in trouble over an illicit substance. It turned out to be hashish, when all Philip tried to buy was a stomach powder. Just another example of how the country'd gone down without the Raj. They'd got the consul out of bed, which he appeared to be sharing with an Indian youth. He was no use at all, and said Philip was a fool. Philip, quite understandably, called the consul a raving poufter. The man then behaved abominably and showed Philip the door by the back of his collar. It transpired too late that the youth was a doctor attending the consul who thought he had influenza. If people don't communicate, what do you expect?

So they'd moved smartly on to Hong Kong. Philip rode the ferry all day. Jan didn't like the shops, but she sat on benches and watched the Chinese. It was very cultural. The children had no backs to their knickers because they don't get potty trained properly. Clear proof they're not like us. Jan couldn't say what they planned to do next.

Si was selective with his telepathic waves. He assured Brigid there'd be none of the itinerants he so disliked on the sites. Neither, it transpired were there to be any totally committed New Agers who might challenge his special qualities as leader. The followers intruded into the calm of Highmoor House over the following week. Dessi was excited and put flowers in all the bedrooms. He selected books for appropriate bedside reading, searching through the Morrow's shelves and the small pile in the van. Since he didn't know exactly who was coming, he chose the Readers' Digest version of Gibbon's *Decline and Fall, The Tale of Peter Rabbit,* Delia Smith's *Cooking for One,* and *Jonathan Livingston Seagull.* He put a notice on the front lawn to discourage the parking of vans.

Duncan arrived by motor cycle wearing black leather, the tough image softened by a turquoise chiffon scarf billowing round his head. 'Sweetie,' he said, 'I've been on the road for five hours. Blown to bits. Show me the bathroom.'

'Sorry,' said Si, watching Duncan trotting neatly up the staircase. 'He's an accountant. Really useful to know. He's only like this out of the office.' Si went out to inspect the motor bike, a Harley Davidson, it didn't measure up to anything like his old Ducati.

When she got used to him, Brigid regarded Duncan as house trained. He left the bath clean, though smelling strongly of magnolia. He was happy to cook and was finicky about his sauces. He washed clothes every day and he told Brigid about a man called Paul who painted soilscapes, a towering genius. Unrecognized. Duncan embraced the New Age because he needed to untrammel himself from the anxieties of other people's money.

Two days later Ogden and Chloe arrived. Ogden wore a suit that draped across his slight frame, scarcely touching. 'Either Armani,' said Si, 'or something his mother ran up.'

'We told them at the office we were on a spiritual sabbatical,' giggled Chloe. 'They looked at us in quite a new light.'

'Set us apart,' agreed Ogden.

Si glanced at Brigid. 'They come from all walks.' He was apologetic.

'They look like people who put the loo lid down,' said Brigid. 'People who are anxious not to offend. A neurotic tendency, but an excellent characteristic when *en masse*.' She went to the kitchen to assemble a chickpea paella. Duncan came to help. 'I'll do you a *mélange* of grape and fig with just a soupçon of cardamom all in a raspberry coulis. Could I borrow your pinny?'

With the dawn came Magda. She stood on the lawn and sang with the waking birds. She was enveloped in layers of many colours and textures, and much hung round with chunky beads.

'How did *she* get to know?' Si asked.

'Must have picked up the telepathy,' said Dessi. 'She *said* she was a mystic. Now we know.'

'Get rid of her. I'm getting bad vibes.'

'You're jealous,' said Dessi. 'She has the gift.'

'Will you come in and have some breakfast?' Brigid called. They stood at the front door unnoticed. Brigid walked tentatively towards her and touched her arm. Magda stopped singing and smiled towards the sky. Then scarcely glancing at her, waved Brigid away with one hand, and glided into the house. She continued up the staircase as if on casters. She moved dreamily from room to room without a single word to anyone.

Brigid wondered if she had a hangover and didn't want to jar her head.

'See what the New Age can do for you,' said Ogden, impressed, as she glided past his bed.

'The daft old bat's on medication,' said Si.

Reginald arrived in a caravan. He was of indeterminate age and wore a thick red-checked woollen shirt, made famous by lumberjacks. His first task was to empty the Elsan down the outside loo. It took eleven flushes, and Reginald was not a steady pourer. Brigid was grateful Dessi sorted out the consequences.

'He's usually very practical,' said Si. 'Good with a hammer and nails.'

'So I would imagine,' said Brigid, handing Dessi a bottle of disinfectant.

'Seven. The magic number. I'm looking for seven,' said Si. 'Six disciples only, counting Dessi. I don't feel complete. I may have to include you, Brigid.'

'I hope there won't be any more,' said Brigid. 'There's only one bedroom left and Perdita may turn up.'

'Perdita?' said Dessi. 'Really?'

'If she lives in the commune she may improve. Sense

the interactive spirit,' Si didn't sound especially optimistic.

'I'm not footing the bill for this lot,' said Brigid.

'Dessi?' Si said.

'Ask Duncan. That's what he's good at. Money.' Dessi was getting more sensible. He'd done well with the outside loo. It was now pristine. He'd spoken to Reginald about future plans for his Elsan.

'Absolutely. Duncan will sort it all out,' agreed Si. 'You see, Brigid? You can't expect me to be grubbing round after money at a time like this.'

'I'll fix it with Duncan,' said Dessi, and went to find him.

Brigid put soda bread in the range, scrubbed carrots, whisked eggs and browned butter. She felt less empty, preparing food for a house full of strange people, serving their needs, creating a pleasure for them. She even felt comfortable with Duncan chopping mint on the table behind her, preparing a sorbet, and quietly humming 'La Vie en Rose'. He wore a blue butcher's apron and his little round spectacles twinkled.

'What's in all this for you, Duncan?' Brigid stopped caring about herself with this crowd around. Perfection was impossible. Her ego was receding. Reluctantly she became part of the flow.

'Got me down for a seedy club life, had you?'

'No. The gourmet and the communal stew pot seem at odds.' She looked at his manicured nails, the fastidious way he held the knife.

'I usually look for a nice little B and B to sleep on bypass days. A day shift up a tree is one thing. Washing in a bucket is quite another.'

'So why do it?'

Duncan chopped mint for a full minute, and Brigid gave up expecting an answer.

'I'm not questioned with *them*,' he said. 'There's nothing you have to fit into.'

'I know what you mean.' She smelled her hands, perfumed with garlic, olive oil, frying, toast, warmth, tarragon, and felt a semblance of tranquillity. She might, she thought, be perfectly happy living here for ever.

'They do a frightfully nice carpaccio of swordfish at the San Lorenzo,' said Chloe at dinner that evening. 'It's so lovely to feel free of luxury,' she simpered waving her spoon over Duncan's soup of spiced parsnip and apple, crunchy with a hint of shallot.

Ogden, who'd explained already he was currently *with* her, said, 'I'm a Roux man myself.' He wore a black silk collarless shirt, girded round the waist like a Cossack.

Duncan glowered. 'Subtle flavours are lost on most people. You obviously missed the teeniest and utterly sophisticated splattering of vodka.' He fastidiously put the tips of left thumb and forefinger together to show the exactitude of the flavour balance.

Reginald shovelling up beignets of ceps and fromage frais, said, 'I don't suppose I could get my duvet in your washing machine, could I? I haven't found a big enough one for four years.'

'The washing machine here is exceptionally small,' said Brigid. 'Would you like some more rice, Magda?'

Magda dragged her gaze back to the present, and eventually located Brigid. She held up her hands expressively and gave a resigned smile, knowing and helpless at the same time.

'Is that a yes or a no?'

Magda repeated the exercise. Brigid put down the serving spoon. She asked, 'Any of you been on the by-pass protest?'

'Course we have,' said Ogden. 'Took a picnic only last Sunday. Had a great day out. Really part of the flow, weren't we, Chloe?'

'I had to be in Geneva,' said Duncan. 'Or I'd have been there, trying to get manhandled by all those lovely security guys.'

'Reginald?'

'The goat died. I had to dispose of it.'

No-one bothered to ask Magda.

Si stood up. 'Welcome,' he said and raised his glass. It was their first dinner assembled all together now that Reginald had arrived. Si made a trip to the cellar with his forged key and come up with a Meursault that would suit Duncan but not be a waste on the others.

The disciples raised their glasses in return, all except Magda who was licking her nails to make them shine. Reginald slurped enthusiastically and held out his glass for more. Duncan shuddered. His first sip hadn't yet reached his soft palette.

'I'm planning an *experience* for the day after tomorrow,' said Si. 'Like to get your responses to this.'

Magda felt the need to lie down on the floor in front of the sideboard.

'Bit of a do, then?' Reginald said. 'Do you wish me to make the van available for toilet facilities?'

Si tried to wither him with a look but Reginald was naturally buoyant. 'Bring your own paper,' he said. 'Not coloured.'

Brigid caught Si's eye, and he looked away.

There was the sound of a car on the drive. Brigid

recognized the jangle of loose parts. Looking out of the window, she saw Perdita climbing clumsily out of the small car, thrusting herself forward as if all her limbs were stiff. Brigid ran into the hall.

Perdita stood in the doorway, a small holdall on the step beside her, arms down by her sides. She made no attempt to disguise the change to her figure. 'Sorry,' she said. 'I'm really sorry, Mum.'

'Perdita. Oh.'

'Yes, Mum. 'Fraid so.'

'Why didn't you tell me?'

'I guess I sort of hoped it would go away.' She ran forwards. 'Mum . . .'

Brigid clasped her pregnant daughter to her and fancied she felt the flutter of life against her own stomach.

They went indoors to the kitchen. Si was refilling the coffee jug. He wasn't pleased with the aspiritual attitudes of his flock, Reginald's and Magda's in particular. The dirty plates were still in the dining-room.

'Out, if you don't mind,' said Brigid abruptly, and pointed with her thumb to the door.

'Wait a minute. This is my house . . . Hey. Do we have some sort of a problem here?'

'Out,' said Brigid again and filled the kettle.

'Fan*tas*tic,' said Si. 'You make seven. Seven disciples. Welcome, Perdita. Perceive those vibrations?'

'Get out,' said Brigid and advanced on him menacingly. Si backed away, and gave a happy wave as he disappeared through the door. Perdita sat morosely at the table, her chin in her hands.

'What's he like . . . your boyfriend?' Brigid asked gently, coming to sit down beside her.

'There isn't one.'

'The father . . . ?'

'It really doesn't matter now.'

'Jez?'

'No.'

'But he would be . . . traceable?'

'Yeah, of course. What do you think I am. Go with strangers, or something?'

'No, well. Sorry. You must understand this is a bit of a surprise.'

'I suppose you're thinking, what will your friends say? What will Jennifer and Murray think? They'll be able to be *really* sorry for you now, won't they?' Her face was twisted up with fear and with self-loathing.

Brigid took hold of her hands. 'None of that has entered my mind. I don't care what they think.'

'They won't know, so you're OK.'

'I won't mind if they *do* know. I'd have minded once. I admit it. Desperately.'

'Are you shocked?' asked Perdita, on the one hand distressed and needing comfort, but on the other, still clinging to her ability to cause pain, and exercise power. 'Do you think I should have got rid of it?'

'No.'

'I thought it would make me different. That was really stupid.'

'There are *better* reasons.'

'What are you feeling then?'

'Sorry you didn't tell me sooner. Worried you're suffering. Happy something wonderful will happen to you, if you let it be wonderful.'

'Can I have it here?'

'Of course. We'll make arrangements. I'm not sure what.'

'Mum, thanks.' Perdita put her head on the table and started to cry. She cried for half an hour, on and off. Si came in once, and went away with a half bottle of vodka. He patted Perdita kindly on the shoulder. 'Seven. What a girl.'

'It's not *him*, is it?'

'For goodness sake, Mum. You're getting a father complex.'

The shock of discovering Perdita was pregnant made Brigid realize she was getting over the shock of the funeral. As with Perdita, there'd been no warning, though perhaps some hints she'd chosen to ignore. There was the lack of love-making, the over-fastidiousness, but Rupert was always a man to keep space around himself.

Rupert died on the Monday. Luckily the heart attack hadn't come while he was driving. It was during the night when he got up to go to the loo. She heard the fall, and had gone half asleep to see if he'd hurt himself. Even then, she was too late.

She put a blanket round him. She tried the kiss of life. She banged hard on his chest, but she knew without any doubt it was useless. She looked at his face still handsome in death, and struggled to wake up from the nightmare. Brigid slipped on a shirt and trousers, and sat beside him on the landing waiting for the ambulance, holding his hand. There were no feelings of pain yet, only a nightmarish emptiness.

In the ambulance, the paramedics tried to perform a miracle, and Brigid felt it was rude to tell them it was a waste of resources. Rupert had left her. Only she, who was so close to him, could know this. Rupert was no longer there, only his body, as a stranger. Being so fastidious he'd have hated his dead body left behind.

It was five o'clock in the morning that they came and told her gently what she already knew. She took a cab home, made some tea, and sat drinking it in the dark. Later, she rang up all the necessary people. Her friends told her that she was being wonderfully brave.

Rupert always wanted to be buried, which surprised Brigid, because cremation is far tidier. She'd have thought he'd hate the idea of his body rotting in a box in the ground, decaying, smelling.

She took care with how she dressed for the service, not out of pride, but as a tribute to Rupert. She wanted him to be proud of her. She bought a new wool coat, black and very straight, which was an extravagance, because black didn't suit her, and she wasn't likely to wear it often. She found a soft hat that pulled down, covering all her hair. Her bones were accentuated and her eyes looked larger in the stark landscape of her face. The black was relieved only with a heavy, cream silk scarf that she wore as a cravat, and pinned with a gold tie pin that Rupert was given at twenty-one. He never used it. He wasn't a tie pin sort of man.

The church was full, but the faces weren't in focus. Brigid was contained and protected in a vacuum. She felt nothing. She knew she'd grieve only when this was over, when she was alone. As yet, she was untouched.

She didn't notice the youth until the coffin was lowered into the ground. Only when he stepped forward did she see him.

Brigid held Perdita as the sobbing subsided. She held her as the breathing grew steadier, as Perdita felt the safety of a mother's caring. Brigid felt a sense of release that at last she could bear to recall that moment at the funeral. The memory had been locked away out of sight, out of her conscious thinking for over a year.

'Will you knit?' Perdita asked. 'I think I might do a cardigan. Something very small.'

'Have you seen a doctor?'

'Just once. Some old goat. You could see he thought I was dirt. I'll have to find someone up here, won't I?'

'I'll ask Aeneas. I think there's a Doctor Withers. He'll know the best place for you to go.'

'Do you see much of Aeneas?'

'Just about the village mostly.'

'I'll never forgive Daddy, you know. Had you guessed?'

'You keep asking that.'

'You must have thought . . . or something.'

What a beautiful man was what Brigid first thought. He stood at the graveside in a black mac, the belt tied in a knot like a girdle, although it had a buckle. He wore no tie to his white shirt. His fair hair was too long at the back, and very straight. Everything about him was pale apart from his clothes. His eyes were so light a blue they appeared opaque, impenetrable. His skin was ashen, faintly scarred with chaste pock marks, romantic brands, a skin with texture, a skin to touch with compassion. He held five white roses.

It's for the widow to cast the first flowers or a symbolic handful of earth on the coffin, and Brigid held tawny roses, *their* colour, together with three green hellebores from the garden. They'd been in the Hebron glass vase all morning, a secret and private message to Rupert. Each tawny rose landed with a soft plop on the coffin. She dropped the hellebores last, at the end of the coffin, nearest to his head, nearest to where his mind had been.

As Brigid moved back from the edge of the grave, the youth stepped forward and cast his white roses onto the pale oak. The flowers landed on top of the hellebores, bisecting their line, and the last one slipped down the side of the coffin, undeniably closer to Rupert. As the man looked down into the chasm of the grave, tears ran down his face.

'Oo, ya bugger,' said Perdita, standing beside her mother and clasping her cold hand in the chill of the graveyard.

Brigid was unaware that those around were looking at each other, some knowingly. Later they'd say Rupert had always been too camp. Jennifer stepped forward and grasped Brigid's arm in a gesture of support. Unconsciously, Brigid shook her off. She couldn't stop staring at the youth, at his face, at the face Rupert knew. The face Rupert may have even loved. She could see why. She knew that when the vacuum around her left, she'd feel jealous, and wondered briefly, if it would've been worse if this was a woman.

True to the elegant person in a black coat, silk scarf and gold pin, someone who didn't feel remotely like Brigid, she wondered if she should ask him back to the house for the buffet.

As they walked to the car park, Brigid said in a general way, 'I hope some of you will come back to the house.' She couldn't stop herself looking towards the youth. She didn't even know his name. It was good manners. It was how Rupert would have behaved.

As she approached the funeral car, he came up and said, 'Obviously I won't come back. But could I come and see you some time?'

'I don't think so,' said Brigid.

'I loved him, you know.'

'So did I,' she said, and got into the car.

'Was Dad like *that*?' Perdita demanded on the way back to the house.

'I don't really know,' said Brigid.

Brigid surprised herself by not clearing the dining-room. The followers had taken themselves off to bed without making any attempt to wash up. The debris of the meal was still there when Brigid came down the next morning. Magda, who was upright again, was swilling one of her layers in the sink.

Brigid felt like an animal let out of a byre, free to graze the summer upland pastures. She'd faced the unfaceable, she'd confronted what had happened at the funeral. She'd accepted Perdita's situation. There was nothing left to fear. It was liberating. 'Soap powder under the sink,' she said helpfully.

Magda smiled mysteriously out of the window.

'Are you OK? Do you need any help with anything?'

Magda held up her scarf to the window and watched the light filter through. 'Looks like silk,' she said. 'An illusion you know.'

'Mmm.'

Magda turned, and the wet scarf dripped on the floor, a tiny April shower on the vinyl tiles. 'You *must* hang onto it.'

'Onto what?'

'The illusory. The only way to endure.'

'Maybe,' said Brigid.

Magda wound the wet scarf round her neck, took off a bolero and put that in the water. Eventually she went outside to dry in the breeze.

The day was sunny, but not humid. After driving round for a while without talking about either the past or the future. Brigid and Perdita had a pub lunch. Brigid knew she had to stay calm and ask no questions, make Perdita feel everything was normal. In the afternoon they drove back to the village and left the car there. Brigid was not at all certain that the washing up would be done, so they went for a walk, down through the village and up on the road towards the next one, where Brigid hadn't been before. There were cowslips and primroses on the bank and hedge bottoms, and apple blossom and wallflowers in the gardens of the cottage. Northumbria had a well-groomed countryside.

'I'm not a pauper any more,' said Brigid. 'Dad's will's settled. I heard last week.'

'So all the ends are tied up.'

'Except one. I regret not meeting that man. I wish I knew what he's like. I don't even know his name.'

'Probably for the best.'

'It's unfinished. It's as if I can't put it all away until I know.'

'You're too orderly, Mum. Why cause yourself more grief?'

'Sometimes I think grief is what I didn't have. Grief for Rupert. I sometimes think it was for our life. It was so harmonious. It was so creative, Perdita.'

'Cold, you mean.'

Brigid didn't ask what she meant. She knew. She felt only relief that she'd changed. The hugely protective love she suddenly felt for Perdita, with pain all mixed up within it, wasn't cold. It was searing, hot like blood, alive, savage and ruthless as nature itself. She remembered what Aeneas said about the Celtic goddess; Brigid was not always a maiden, but a mother and enabler. She'd come into her namesake this time, that was for sure.

‘Are you getting over Dad a bit. The shock and everything?’

‘How can I mourn something I never had? I grieve because I never *had* what I thought was there.’ Brigid hadn’t expected it would be Perdita to whom she confessed. It was wrong to burden her. ‘Come on. Five more minutes then we’ll go back for a nice cup of tea.’

They both stopped when they saw the cottage through the trees. The *For Sale* notice hung crooked on the gate post.

‘Magic,’ said Perdita. ‘It can’t be real. Anyone living there?’

‘Doesn’t look like it. We could see.’

The cottage had clearly been empty for some time. There were cobwebs at the windows and dead flies on the sills. The large room at the front looked over the lane. The kitchen was tacked on at the back, like a sty. There was a range far too big for it, and a rough wooden table in the middle. Everything was filthy. Brigid guessed there were two bedrooms at the front. From the variety of pipes above the kitchen it seemed there might be a bathroom with a loo.

‘Aunt Roo lived in a cottage like that,’ Brigid said.

‘We could paint everything white,’ said Perdita.

They looked at each other, and there was nothing to discuss.

‘The Morrows ought to be back before September. You still want the baby to be born up here?’

Perdita nodded, her eyes on the tops of the trees, locating a singing bird. It was a wren.

Brigid knew this was where she could make a nest for Perdita, a nest where she’d no longer be cold. Aunt Roo had given her self-worth in a cottage like this. She would do the same for her child. Brigid was a woman who could accept memory, who no longer deceived herself. She was a woman who could make decisions.

When they got back to Highmoor House they saw Jennifer and Murray through the sitting-room door, sitting primly on the sofa drinking strong tea from mugs supplied by Dessi. He also provided biscuits. He'd found a packet on the top shelf in the pantry, and the chocolate coating had a white bloom to it.

'Whoops,' said Perdita.

'Visitors,' Dessi whispered, jerking his head towards the room. He looked uncomfortable with them.

'Where are the others?'

'Gone to Lindisfarne. All except Magda. I couldn't stand being with them today. They should be back by now. I think they've missed the tide.'

'Let's hope so. Is the washing up done?'

'Almost.'

Without any rush of warmth Brigid went to her friends.

'Darling,' said Jennifer, 'we're passing through on our way home from Edinburgh. I said to Murray, "We must call in and see Brigid." We'd have let you know but we didn't have the phone number. How *are* you?'

'Lovely to see you,' said Brigid automatically. 'I'm much better.'

'Who is that strange young man?'

'Jan's son has come home for a while. That's his friend.'

'Hope you'll be all right with them here,' said Jennifer.

'Looks a lay-about to me,' said Murray, whose special talent was seeking out the obvious.

'Si has healing qualities.'

Perdita came into the room behind her and there was total silence. Brigid could see Jennifer twisting her head round to see if she were wearing a wedding ring. 'Ah,' she said, 'my poor Brigid.' She walked over and tried to put her arms around her.

'Honestly, Jennifer. It's not "poor Brigid" at all. I'm coming to terms with my life. Isn't it wonderful that Perdita's having a child? I feel so close to her. Don't you think she looks lovely?'

'Yes, of course,' said Jennifer. 'You look lovely, Perdita. Doesn't she Murray?' For once Murray felt unable to say what was crystal clear to him, and lacked the imagination to think of anything else. He nodded and swallowed.

'Well then,' said Jennifer, eager to get away from the subject. 'How much longer are you staying up here?'

'I don't know. The Morrows have postponed their return again.'

'So you've got to stay up here even *longer*?'

'I like it.'

'Oh.'

'You'll stay to supper?'

'We'd better be going. Only popped in.'

Brigid walked with them to their car. Unfortunately, Magda was sleeping by the gate, propped up against the post. With commendable tact, Jennifer said not a word and gave the faintest of smiles.

'Well I never,' said Murray, but was unable to finish because of the pressure of Jennifer's stiletto heel on his instep. He negotiated the cluttered gateway carefully.

Brigid watched the car drive away down the empty road that eventually led back to Wimbledon. 'Thank you,' she whispered. 'Thank you for showing me.' Before going inside, she swung Magda's legs round so she was no longer sticking out over the drive, but tucked safely into the flower bed. Si, driving the van home, might not be as careful as Murray.

With a sense of release, and to celebrate, she raided the cellar and opened a bottle of champagne, a lot of which she drank while scrubbing new potatoes.

Solstice

There are places in the Celtic landscapes that retain a power thought lost. This was true of islands and places where great goodness existed. If a relationship with the elements was secured by the spirit, then a sacred place was established. The Celts knew they could return to such places and, by ritual, momentarily realign the connection between spirit and elements. Other places have remained holy throughout time because they were gateways between this world and the other. Here people could communicate with the spirit world, which was not so much another place, but a coexisting world overlaying the material one. Alongside a burial mound particularly there was likely to be a gateway, and many claimed to have seen spirit forms beside Celtic graves at the time of the solstice or the equinox. Such places were gateways centuries ago, and nothing has happened to the land to change that. Only people have changed, in that they have lost the power to be aware of holiness in the natural world.

Time was an element as well as a space in the Celtic mind, and at the turning points of the sun, and at the return or departure of the seasons the moment was auspicious. Life was perpetually marked by the changes of the earth, by its growth and continual renewal. At the summer solstice the sun was at the highest point in the northern heavens, the beneficence of the sun god was at its most generous, and it was then that the ancient people came out to praise him.

They also knew he was about to change his path, and they lit fires and strew flowers to remind him to return again.

The Celtic Way, A.B. Westlake

Dessi cleaned the van in honour of the summer solstice and of the Coming Together. All the followers except Duncan would journey in it. Duncan disliked travelling by anything other than his own machine. They had trouble loading Magda into the van as she'd fallen in love with the sycamore tree, and stood clasping it in her arms. They prised her off it, and she stood resolutely gazing back at the tree with tears in her eyes under the last of the stars.

'She needs her medication changing,' said Si. 'You take the other leg, Reginald.' They heaved her into the van and battened her down by having Chloe and Ogden sit either side on her layers of skirts. She sang 'On Top of Old Smokey' softly to herself for the whole journey.

'Bewick Hill will be much better than Stonehenge,' enthused Si. 'Everyone goes *there*, and the ambience gets lost. You've got to have space. You've got to have air. Come on, Brigid.'

'I don't like Druids,' she said.

'Druids are out. Gone. *Passé*. Absolutely no Druids, I promise. I'm not asking for bare flesh either. Even from the nubile. You've done the picnic. You're providing the loaves and fishes. A vital role. Why not be part? Aeneas is coming, by the way.'

'OK. I'll join the pilgrimage.'

'It's not a pilgrimage. That's old hat too. It's a Coming Together from all quarters. Yes. A Coming Together.'

'Then what?'

'A revelation? Miracles? Who knows?'

'Will you need your surfboard for any of those?'

Si ignored her. 'Where's Perdita? She's one of seven. We need her fruitfulness. Come *on*. We must be there by dawn.'

Brigid wore the Celtic brooch Aeneas had given her, anchoring a green silk scarf tucked into the neck of her shirt. Perdita, coming downstairs at last, said 'That's nifty, Mum.' She looked heavy and shapeless in a denim tent shape. 'I don't think I'll come. I'm just a lump.'

'No you're not. You've got a glow. Your skin has never been better.'

'I feel ugly.'

'Here, you borrow the scarf,' said Brigid. She draped it round Perdita's neck, so that the ends flowed free, and secured it with the Celtic brooch. 'There. Something at the neck distracts the eye from the bulge.'

Perdita looked in the hall mirror. 'I suppose I don't look *that* bad.'

'You look really good.'

'Come *on*,' shouted Si.

Aeneas and Brigid followed in his car. Alys took up the back seat.

'We want no extra space in cars,' said Brigid. 'After the Coming Together, there'll be a Going Away. No-one else is going to jump on the bath and washing machine bandwagon.'

They drove in the dark towards the Cheviots.

'Didn't expect to see you,' said Brigid.

'There's a wonderful view.'

'Why Bewick Hill?' Brigid asked.

'There's a bronze age burial ground. Only a small

bump on the hill.' The rest of the way they drove in silence.

They parked the car and van at Old Bewick, a small grey stone hamlet nestling comfortably at the foot of Bewick Hill. There were already three cars parked on the grass bank, two of which might belong to farm workers. The third was a Capri, an individual spray job of pale aqua. 'Good. Good,' said Si. 'Jamie's arrived already.'

'Got the food Brigid?'

'Yes, but I'm not carrying any of it.'

'Dessi,' said Si. 'See to it. Organize.' Si was flushed, excited at the prospect of the dawn.

'Duncan and Reginald can do it between them.' Dessi had a bag of his own to deal with, which was gear for Si.

'Ra*ther*,' said Duncan.

'Not bleeding likely,' said Reginald. 'I've got the rope and a torch.' He was put out that the offer of his Elsan facility had been rejected.

'What are those for?'

'I'm a practical man.'

They walked through a gate and up a cobbled track that led towards Bewick Hill. They were climbing all the time through bracken and sheep grazing terrain. As they got further up, the grazing gave way to heather, and there were no longer any sheep. Perdita complained her feet were hurting. Dessi walked behind her, occasionally taking her elbow on the steeper bits. Perdita was hot and grumpily shook him off.

Magda was a surprisingly sprightly walker, having forgotten the sycamore tree. She strode out sturdily, but soon got out of breath. She sat on a rock, and as Brigid passed, reached out and caught hold of her sleeve. 'Sit with me a minute,' she said.

'It *is* a bit steep,' said Brigid, looking back.

In the dark, Magda leaned forward, staring curiously into her face. 'I see the fates,' she whispered. 'There is a crossroads.'

'Oh.' Brigid was polite.

'Simon is jealous. You know that. I have the sight.'

'A gift.'

'I see the crossroads. There are two paths.'

'Right.'

'You understand?'

'Not really.'

Magda gathered her layers and rose like a scarecrow from the rock. 'You will, my dear.' She didn't wait for Brigid but rushed off at a pace, and collapsed again onto the next available rock.

'Leave her,' said Reginald. 'She'll blow along later. Difficult to lose Magda. Like a plastic bag against the windscreen.' He was following their progress on a map encased in a milky polythene envelope that hampered clarity. He had to tip it in various directions to pick up the light from his torch.

'You're taking this very seriously, Reginald.' Brigid caught him up.

'Respected for my thorough approach, aren't I?'

'A strange partner to Aquarian fluidity.'

'Fluidity's their problem,' said Reginald. 'I look after the plumbing. Metaphorically. Si overflows from time to time. I sort him out.'

'Yes?'

'He has excesses. Got arrested in Banbury for vagrancy. Pleased as a randy Tom he was at that. But he needed me to get him out. Wrote a reference to the magistrates in copperplate. That did the trick. You need a bit of class when you're in court.'

Eventually they saw some ruins at the top of a slope. The roofless walls seeped sadness and loss, like Top Withens dominating the hills where the Brontës walked.

'That's Blawearie,' said Aeneas. 'Just three cottages. Been derelict for decades.'

'We don't go that far,' said Si. 'Left at the track just before the stream.'

They reached an untidy rectangular pile of stones that was the burial mound. It seemed too casual and vulnerable to have survived in the exact form for three thousand years. 'This is it,' said Si, determined, so there was no room for doubt.

It was then Brigid saw the youth.

He stood in the grey darkness on the far side of the mound, one of five people. She recognized him instantly, though she'd seen him only once. She could never forget that face. He looked as sad as he had beside Rupert's grave. And as pale. *Oh what can ail thee, knight at arms?* He was a man of damp sedges, silent birds and spent harvest. He had little in common with the summer, or with the sunrise. She instinctively stepped back.

No longer in his black raincoat, he still looked beautiful. He approached Si, and shook him courteously by the hand. There was no intimacy between them. Si saw no reason to introduce him to the others. *This* must be Jamie. He stood back, fastidiously apart, scarcely glancing at the seven disciples now gathering at the mound.

Brigid stood back as well, standing behind Aeneas. It was already growing lighter. It was almost dawn. She wanted to watch this youth, before he knew she was there, watch him before he might feel he had a part to act.

Her reaction was negative, she felt hatred and jealousy and anger. She could speak to him if she wanted, if she dared. It was an amazing coincidence he should turn up here. Then she realized the link was back in Wimbledon. If *she* knew the Morrows, and Si Morrow knew *him*, Rupert could easily have met him too. She glanced across the small crowd, and saw Magda with the hint of a smile on her nebulous face.

Dessi watched Brigid. Each day now, his mind seemed clearer. Brigid had a strange expression. She was looking at Jamie. The pieces danced in his mind, lively with all their possibilities. Dessi thought he *almost* understood.

'Ready?' Si called. This was not a guitar and dancing occasion. This was his most serious gathering yet. He expected help from an etheral force. He found a flat rock, which he designated as an altar, though he contested the name. 'It's the Centring,' he said.

'Can't you all feel the presence?' Magda cried. 'Only the finest of veils between us now.' Her chest was heaving with the uphill climb, but it looked like emotion.

'No they can't,' said Si. 'Not yet.'

'I see a man rising out of that earth in a . . .'

'Dessi,' said Si.

'Reginald,' said Dessi, pointing to Magda.

'There, my love. There, there, little one,' said Reginald, as if he were talking to a self-willed cow. 'You take a hold of this piece of rope. We'll go with it and see where it leads.' Magda obediently followed as he led her away.

Four more people followed up the hill, random hikers, possibly insomniac. They hung about, wondering if this were some ancient rite, even optimistic of a free breakfast.

From Dessi's bag Si produced vases, flowers and a plastic bottle of water. 'Water is central,' he said. 'Yellow irises for the sun god. White tulips for the moon goddess.' He put the flowers in the vases. 'Now make a circle around us and I'll initiate you into the world of the spirit. Spread out more,' he said. 'Watch it, Dessi, you'll fall off that rock if you go any further.'

Dessi said, '*Si? Initiate?* You said we find our own inner life.'

'I know better now. Right?'

'We didn't used to have gods and goddesses.'

'We've got them now. Shut up, Dessi.'

'It's not right. It's getting complicated.'

Perdita stood up. 'Can I be your handmaiden?'

'We only have virgins. That's why there aren't any,' said Si. 'Sit down, please, Perdita. I'll lead the meditation, right?'

'You said no one could *know*,' said Dessi.

'But I *do*,' said Si softly.

Brigid avoided sitting opposite Jamie, and he'd not yet seen her. He wasn't interested in anyone around him, staring absently at the ground. Duncan, on the other hand, brightened up considerably and pushed into the circle next to him.

Aeneas grinned at Brigid, his asymmetrical smile, eyebrows shooting off in unexpected directions, and spread out his jacket for her to sit on. 'I've been huffy.'

'It doesn't matter.'

'Can't do that,' called Si. 'She won't get properly earthed.' Brigid hotched off it onto the grass.

Si sat cross-legged before them. He held up his hands so the followers could receive energy from him.

'Feel our union with the earth at the dawn of the sun. The goddess of plenitude and generosity, gives us more energy than at any other time. The sun is with us for the longest day. Feel the unity and the harmony. Reach out and find the harmony within ourselves. Recognize the oneness of creation. Experience the energy that is the power for good. The power of life itself.'

Chloe giggled. She rehearsed describing the scene to her colleagues in the typing pool at Roosters Corporate Financing. She might gain more kudos by entertaining stories than through spiritual detachment.

'We'll wait,' said Si, 'until the negative force diminishes.'

Chloe stuffed her fist in her mouth. Ogden, in Austrian climbing shorts, gave her a withering look. How would he ever get due respect from the young men who dealt in noughts per second at Roosters Corporate Financing if he had a partner who was a twit? He worked hard at being different from the herd, eccentric and enviable. Magda, still clinging to her rope, was led back as her peceptions had subsided. She beamed at Si like a luminous cow, channelling divine energy from her own mystic source.

Si had the right voice for leading meditation. It wasn't his words they listened to, it was the resonance, the inflections and the timbre. The followers became aware of the *moment* and moved away from material distraction, emptied their minds of trivia. They felt the cold of the earth enter into them, and the stirring of energy as the sun inched over the horizon. They listened to their breath. They let the world glide by. They discerned the source of all energy and dew upon it.

Brigid always relaxed when Si did the meditation thing. It helped to feel the ebb and the flow of breath. How wise of the ancients to worship the sun, so transparently benevolent, so obviously the source of well-being. How sensible to have worshipped an object so visible, instead of the ambivalent *truths* that later religions introduced.

She, so much stronger now, could face the past. She was apart from what had gone before and could see her marriage for the empty shell it was. It was the organization that fulfilled her, but she'd created only a shell fashioned out of perfection. There was understanding between her and Rupert, but no passion. There never was, right from the beginning. No lust. Only a sense of being rescued. Perhaps he'd felt the same and been grateful.

She sloughed off the chains of memory that restricted her. She emerged like a snake from a desiccated skin to be gleaming fresh in the sunlight. She was free of memory because she was no longer slave to it. Neither was she afraid to confront Jamie. She would speak to him when Si was through.

When the sun finally broke free from the horizon, Si jumped up and raised his palms to the sky. He gestured others to do the same. They stood wondering at the beauty and the power of the circle in the sky and were changed. They were realigned to the core of the natural world.

'Bless Gaia,' shouted Si.

'Bless Gaia,' most answered, meekly as lambs, though not Aeneas or Brigid. Dessi too, kept his mouth closed. Magda shook her head in wonder. Chloe was smirking. Ogden looked dazed. Reginald patted Magda. He missed the goat sometimes. Duncan was looking at the youth. Jamie looked wistful. Whatever Si had summoned moved among them, and they all felt a momentry wonder, a sense outside themselves.

Si looked into their faces. He'd led these people. He'd opened their eyes. He'd been a conduit for the truth. He was exultant. 'Your opportunity, Brigid, to feed the five thousand,' he said, with a flourish as if he'd personally created her for that purpose.

'Nineteen,' said Perdita.

'Same principles,' said Si.

Brigid unpacked loaves of soda bread from the teatowels that were keeping the crusts soft. She put hard-boiled eggs in a dish, and uncorked flasks of coffee. There was a fruit cake to provide the bountiful element, rich in glacé pineapple and candied ginger for plenitude. She used the Centring stone as a table. The followers flocked about her like gannets.

She turned round and in front of her the youth stood, tentative and wary.

'Oh,' said Brigid. They stared at each other with fear and some curiosity.

'I'm sorry. I have to go. I didn't know . . .' He walked away, down the track through the heather.

'Don't leave.'

'Must get on.' Half way down the hill he paused, looked back, but then took off again and disappeared.

Aeneas was watching. 'You know him? He recognized *you*.'

'I met him once.' Brigid shrugged her shoulders.

'Let's take our breakfast up to Blawearie,' said Aeneas. 'Great view.'

The two of them climbed the small incline to reach the smooth turf that once was the gardens of the tiny cottages. Aeneas climbed ahead. His long legs levered easily over the rocks.

He's got a lovely bum, thought Brigid. Neat and athletic.

The trees stunted by the harsh winters had a tranquillity about them now that the weather was benign. The view was all the way to the Cheviot hills over the river Till. There was a personal feel to the earth as if ghosts still wanted to live in this lonely and beautiful place.

'It would change you, living here,' said Brigid.

'And yet they left,' said Aeneas looking back to the ruins. 'I don't know what happened.'

They sat on the grass a discreet yard apart.

Aeneas looked younger and more vulnerable, his hair wispy on the back of his neck. 'Do you miss London?'

'Not so much now. I'm getting my mind round my life.'

'The Celts, you know, believed they could only fully conquer their enemies by possessing their heads, and therefore their thoughts. The habit of collecting heads makes the Celts look gruesome today, but there was a psychological explanation. They needed to encapsulate. It's the same with pain. You have to cut it off from the rest of your life. So it doesn't drag you down.'

Brigid wondered if he were talking about himself or her. Probably both. That's what he'd done with his life with Hilly. Except he'd cut his whole self off. She liked the image of encapsulation. That's how she was dealing with the memory of Rupert. It would always be there. She had to gather the memories up, encase them, put a shell around the pain, not let them spill out all over her life. She must stop the jealousy she'd felt earlier spreading and corrupting. The humiliation of seeing the beautiful young man at the funeral mustn't stain her mind.

'They seemed very wise, the Celts,' she said.

'Fascinating people. My book is about their beliefs, and how they relate to today. I suppose Hilly started me off. Witchcraft goes back to the pagan. Wanted to prove to her it was all ridiculous, but of course, it wasn't. They were certain, like Christians. Like Si.'

'Will it be published?'

'Only if I find my own angle. There are plenty of works on the Celts, more erudite than mine could be.'

'I hope I can read it one day.' Brigid thought that Aeneas, casual in the sunshine, was the very opposite of the aloof *hubby* she'd first seen, drained of warmth, depleted of laughter. He was intelligent. He was kind. He was vulnerable, but the lines round his mouth when he smiled had deepened over the last months. He was attractive. Even if he was untidy. Brigid looked down at the followers, still eating. She spotted Magda who had got her ear to the ground beside the burial mound. She remembered the muttering about cross-roads.

'Will you go to London when the Morrows come back?'

'They keep putting off their return.' She didn't feel yet that she could mention the cottage she might buy. It seemed such a big step in her life. Would Aeneas mistakenly think it had anything to do with him?

He turned round so that he faced her, leaning on his hands behind him. He was watching her and when she looked at him he didn't immediately look away.

'I sometimes wonder what would have happened if I'd been braver at Durham,' he said. It was more a question than a reflection and had nothing to do with Durham.

'You could have been very happy,' she said. 'You wouldn't have been rejected.' She looked at his wide, firm mouth, and his eyes didn't leave her face. They were two people momentarily suspended in time. Soon he would lean towards her.

Perdita climbed the hill to join them. 'I want to go home, Mum. I'm tired.' She pouted and had lost her arrogant posture. At her neck, the Celtic brooch blinked in the sun. Aeneas stared at it.

Perdita put her hand to it and said, 'Isn't it pretty? Mum gave it to me.'

'*Lent* it to you, Perdita,' Brigid said, but already too late.

Aeneas looked at her, disappointed and vulnerable again. This was how he looked as a student. She knew then the present had been more personal even in February than he'd pretended.

He stood up. 'I like it too,' he said and walked down the hill.

'Please let's get this right,' Brigid said running after him. 'I *lent* it to her this morning to cheer her up. I was wearing it myself. She felt plain and I pinned it on her dress.'

'It suits her,' said Aeneas. 'She should keep it.' He added, 'Time to be off.'

Brigid glanced back at the remains of the meal and decided to leave them to it. Si led the rest down Bewick Hill. Magda followed, steadying herself with a hand on his shoulder. He transferred the hand to Reginald, who luckily still had his piece of rope. Dessi was last, clearing up the debris from the picnic, putting it all in a plastic sack. Perdita helped him, stooping down to cull the occasional eggshell or paper cup like Ophelia picking herbs.

When he got back, Aeneas walked Alys all morning on the moors. She was tired before he was. He tried to walk away the bitterness, get rid of the sense of loss that was his life. He might be free now, but that didn't make up for all the wasted years. It didn't make amends for what his life might have been.

Back at his cottage he opened the top drawer of Hilly's chest, and took out the leather purse Hilly'd wanted when she was dying. He opened it and saw the hazel twigs, the ash, the feather and small coloured stones, tools of Hilly's trade. Hilly'd humiliated him, made him feel a fool. Not that it mattered. He took everything outside including the purse and burned them, not among the trees where Hilly worked her spells but on the vegetable plot that was plain honest earth. It was time to be free of what tied him to the past. He burned the purple cloak and the fumes rose black into the sky. He hoped it wouldn't attract the attention of an environmental officer. For an hour, they polluted the air, but when the smoke cleared Aeneas felt that the air was cleaner.

Brigid had given away the brooch, his only present to her. He'd reacted as he always did to any setback, by running away, turning his back, showing he didn't care. He'd never had the guts to go for what he wanted. He could have made it with Roni Carver if he'd had the courage. Someone told him years later that she liked him. Today he'd banished Hilly and her scheming. From now on he would be different.

* * *

Brigid washed her hair and let it dry in the sun. She didn't shape it with the dryer, or sleek it with mousse. It fell as it grew. Rolando would have winced. She was free of her London life and her beautiful home. She was free of old pretentions and assumptions. She was free of Jennifer and Murray. There was more to life than material pleasures. There was magic in the woods. Unfortunately, it looked as if she were free of Aeneas as well.

Si was up early and washed his sap green robes. They flapped on the clothes line like the sails of the fleet about to meet the Armada. Yesterday had been great. Something *had* happened. He felt different. His ideas had been confirmed. He was right. He ate his muesli urgently, constantly glancing across to Brigid. Dessi scrambled an egg.

'My time has come. It's imminent. Do you think so, Brigid?'

'Could be.' Brigid opened the kitchen window and sniffed at the smell of soil. She'd fed the earth and watered it, cleaned it and touched it with love. She'd planted herbs beneath the kitchen window and the smell of them drifted up into the house.

'I'm getting rid of Chloe and Ogden. Not good material. Contaminated. They can't stay. Dessi?'

'Do your own dirty work,' said Dessi.

'Thank *you*. Otherwise it went well. I must plan the next stage. Where's Tara?'

'I thought I recognized one young man yesterday. The one who turned up early. In a funny coloured car.' Brigid spoke lightly.

'Jamie. Yes, you might have seen him around. Same

block of flats as the Onspring in Wimbledon. That's where I met him, anyway. More precisely, at the Thai take-away down the road. I must have dropped in there while they were away. Took him for a city type. He's a playwright though. That's what he says. Bit of a lost soul.'

'Lives in my area, then?' said Brigid, explaining what had seemed an unlikely coincidence. 'Has he gone now?'

'Dunno.'

'He's gone back to London,' said Dessi.

'Didn't seem typical somehow. Artistic perhaps. Not really New Age.' Brigid stayed casual and not particularly interested.

'He's interested in other realms,' said Si. 'I think there was a bereavement. I haven't got round to trying to help him yet.'

'That's a pity.' Brigid smiled and wondered why Dessi looked speculative.

Later that morning the phone rang. 'Is Si there? Have I the right number?'

'He is. You have. Who's that?'

'A friend of his. Jamie. Well, not to bother him now. I'll be seeing him. Right. Thanks.'

'Jamie? Jamie . . .'

Brigid sat on the bottom stair. Was that the voice of the youth at the funeral? She thought so, but couldn't be certain. It was a light voice, not deep, not rough, but certainly not camp. She thought he probably recognized her own crisp tone.

Perdita went back to London. She said she was restless. Brigid took her to catch the eleven-thirty train, and cried as she drove back from the station. She changed her mind when she came to the crossroads and didn't take the turn to Highmoor House. Instead she drove down to the cottage in the woods. It was as peaceful as ever, standing quietly empty, not fretting at its solitude, a haven of peace in the emotional upheaval of the world. Brigid checked the address of the estate agent on the 'For Sale' notice, and went straight to their office in Alnwick.

Lughnasahd

At the beginning of the month we now call August, the Celts celebrated the feast of Lugh on his wedding day. It was the beginning of the Celtic autumn, a time of fruitfulness. Lugh was a raven god, a god of power, some menace and undeniable greatness. He was the bright one, being a smith and so one who forged destiny, a hero and historian, doctor, magician, hero of his own tales, which he sang to the music of his harp.

The Celtic wedding was a pragmatic arrangement. The couple could live together for a year and a day. If by the end of that time the union was not considered satisfactory it could be terminated. What this meant in practical terms we have no means of knowing.

It was an ambiguous time, true to the now Aquarian principle of fluidity and change. While it was fruitful, a time of culmination and harvest, there was always an underlying sense of sacrifice. The price to pay for the harvest was the coming of winter.

It was then that the goddess of three forms, Brigid, was no longer the maiden, but fully the wise woman. She was patron of the poets and gave them her protection, and she was also the healer. She was the mother of memory and in her care resided creative and magical arts.

The Celtic Way, Aeneas B. Westlake

Brigid opened the front door, and sat down in the

middle of the empty living-room. The cottage was hers.

Everything had gone through quickly, there were no other properties involved. She had the money so there was no mortgage. The decision was taken even before the next letter arrived from the Morrows warning of a further postponement of their return due to Philip's happy relationship with the dolphins off the west coast of Australia. He was writing an epic poem that required that he stayed with them another month. He would become a famous ecologist.

Brigid wished Perdita hadn't gone back to London. They could have chosen colours together, but then Perdita never was a nest maker. Brigid didn't tell Aeneas about the cottage, and she didn't know why. Perhaps it was because seeing her as a woman who could afford to buy a cottage on a whim would widen the gap between them, anyway he might not want her to stay in the area. She just didn't know how or what Aeneas thought, especially after the huff over the brooch. Perdita had given it back to her, never realizing the damage her careless words had caused.

Si prepared to go out into the world. Disciples were one thing, but they have their limits. He'd already opened their eyes. He planned a short tour in the autumn, before the winter set in. He must be totally prepared for this. He bought a notebook and made a series of outlines for lectures. There were headings: The goddess; collective consciousness; the lungs of the earth; role of the Shaman; sacred places; keeping the sun alive. These essays would become his gospel. He would put them on Philip's word processor and produce copies. He could hand them out. Dessi made phone calls.

Chloe and Ogden were dismissed. It was acrimonious.

He discussed the tour with his remaining followers with the exception of Magda. 'We'll travel in convoy,' Reginald assured Si. 'Then you needn't worry if the van breaks down.'

'You don't *have* to come. Really,' said Si.

'We could put Magda in a cage,' said Duncan. 'You'd look like Agamemnon returning from Priam with Cassandra.'

'What a pity you've a job to get back to,' said Si.

'You won't like sorting out your own income support,' retorted Duncan.

When Si ran out of headings he doodled a picture of the earth as a woman in a tree, or the sun cradling a child. The lines were elusive, sometimes the image was there, sometimes not. Brigid watched Si over his shoulder as he drew, and he drew for her.

'You *should* have gone to art school.'

'I told you why not.' He sighed 'Perhaps if I had, I wouldn't be shackled with the mission. It's a heavy cross.' He looked up at her, and the expression in his eyes was that of a man beseeching to be set free.

Brigid couldn't think of anything comforting to say, so she fetched him a soothing mug of hot chocolate, and he drank it hunched up beside Hilly's rowan tree.

It was hot and there was no rain for three weeks. Brigid stood on the threshold of the cottage for the first time since it had become hers. She left the door open so she could see across the valley. The sun shimmered on the hill tops, and drained the colours from the trees so that they all looked the same, a soft, pale sage. There was no bustle, no compulsion, there was space to let the soul grow, just for its own sake, and not to achieve anything at all. It was a place where her life would be stripped down to the essentials. A life no longer including sophisticated food, or pleats in skirts, or maintaining Rolando's hair style. There would be room only for the encapsulated nugget of pain that had been with her for more than a year, and for the pool of comfort of Perdita's child to come.

She stood in the one downstairs room, apart from the kitchen, and had already decided to paint the room white. She would have a cream sofa, with a washable cover because of the child being sick all over it. The whole cottage would be white, so that it seemed full of air and light. There'd be pine furniture, plain modern furniture. No antiques. No place for a chaise longue or a Victorian nursing chair. No round wine table or mahogany corner cupboard, and no chairs with cabriole legs. There would be no values of the nineteenth century. Everything would be simple and clean cut, minimalist but with lovely fabrics, perhaps some rugs. She might wash over some of the plain wood with a saxe blue, or perhaps a warm, dark green stain.

This place would banish the past, and in it she would find the person she was to become. She would sit among the trees and feel at one with nature, as Si taught her. His peace he had given her, and soon now she'd be centred, finding her own peace; she would be linked to the earth. What a strange boy he was. He'd glimpsed a truth, and he was trying to pin it down like a dead butterfly, framing it, limiting its horizons, cutting it down to human dimensions.

She would be happy here for happiness's own sake.

The energy would be for living *now*, for Perdita and for the child.

She went up the narrow stairs, and was looking at the front bedroom when she heard a car. She went to the window and saw Jamie's customized aqua Capri. That he should come to her in this place seemed proof that this cottage was meant to be hers.

He climbed elegantly out of his car and stood still when Brigid appeared at the open front door. 'I hope you don't mind me coming. I'll go away if you'd rather.' He was nervously casual, he'd rehearsed the words.

'How did you find me?' Brigid was, in contrast, being unprepared, brusque where she'd have preferred to be aloof.

'Dessi rang me up at home. He said I should come back and talk to you.'

'Dessi? Well now, who'd have thought he'd do that?' She nodded, still ruffled. 'Luckily I have a kettle. I won't be a moment. Find somewhere to sit in the shade.'

She didn't want him in this house. He must stay in the open air, where the memory of what he would tell her would later blow away. There must be no association of him with her sitting-room.

'Perhaps I'm selfish,' said Jamie, when she came out with two mugs, 'but I hate loose ends.' He'd been working on his words again.

'Who's the loose end? You or me?' How dare he presume to take the initiative in this conversation?

'Ah.'

There were two wooden chairs in the garden, and Jamie had put them in the shade of a lime tree. The fragrance came down to them, heavy and sweet. Brigid moved the chairs forward, so the nectar wouldn't drop on them. She was also reluctant to associate this man with anything as beautiful as the scent of lime blossom. She sniffed, determined that she couldn't smell even a trace.

He sat back, apparently relaxed in a white collarless textured shirt, and worryingly tight black jeans, a faint blond growth around his chin. His eyelids were crazed with faint mauve veins, fleetingly feminine. His hands hung loose and elegant over the arms of the wooden chair.

Brigid stared at him, the benevolent peace she'd felt earlier totally fled. But his confident look could not withstand the resentment in her eyes. His gaze slid from her face down to the grass. She noticed then he wasn't relaxed at all. His feet were tensed against the ground, the neck muscles were sharp where they disappeared inside his collar, even though his mouth maintained that easy and composed smile. This man wasn't all he seemed. He was less than she'd imagined. Less powerful. Anger at his being here and catching her unawares turned slowly to curiosity. Intense curiosity had, after all, been her first conscious emotion when she saw him originally. There'd been remarkably little jealousy or anger. Simply because the situation was beyond her understanding. The greatest need had been to know, her main feeling was curiosity.

'I wished I'd spoken after the funeral,' she said, 'but it was too soon. Now I want to know . . . what you were to Rupert. How important. How long he knew you. That sort of thing.'

'I knew him for ten months.'

'OK.' She waited.

'What else do you want me to say?' The elegance began to slip. The youth was thrown now that she began to sound reasonable. He'd been prepared for a storm. For temper. For jealousy. Perhaps that was what he'd come for?

Brigid waved her hands vaguely in front of her, irrelevantly aware he'd admire her well-kept nails. 'Nothing graphic. Nothing specific. But I'd like to know . . . why. Yes, I need to understand why.'

'I thought you knew why.' There was the hint of a sneer.

'Because Rupert was bisexual? I never *knew*. Looking back, and believe me, I've looked back over and over again this last year. Looking back, I must have refused to consider it, but subconsciously, the thought must have lurked even before I saw you. He was so fastidious, so perceptive. He knew how to dress, understood colours. He was spiritual.

'You know, if I'd imagined a lover for him, I'd have expected a bit of rough. Someone quite *different* from himself.' Brigid laughed. She instinctively knew Jamie would understand the rules of women's conversation. If she confessed her thoughts, he would too. She waited. She was the relaxed one now.

Jamie said slowly, 'Rupert was otherwise faithful to you. I was his aberration. He wanted to be a normal husband more than anything.'

'So it was just . . . sex?'

'Not entirely. He needed to talk about it. About being both. He didn't want to be like he was. I was the only time he allowed anything to happen. He was appalled, but he couldn't help himself. He couldn't be gay and leave it at that. I suppose because he was so wonderful I let him talk about you and his home. Others wouldn't. But there was no-one like Rupert. I had to put up with it.'

They'd both been attracted to the same thing. It was the quality of the man, his looks, his uncluttered mind, his kindness without involvement.

Brigid looked closer at the youth, searching out his ambivalence. Yes. Just as his stubbled chin coexisted with his delicate mauve veined eyelids, his poised hands with his tense neck muscles, so generosity was simultaneous with self interest. He was not only reassuring *her*, but making it clear that he, *Jamie*, had been the only man in Rupert's life. Even now, there were parameters to lay out and territory to claim.

Brigid felt her ascendancy. She played the conversation as if it had strings beneath her fingers. 'Why couldn't he talk to me? We were close.' She drew her forehead into a puzzled frown. There were admissions to extract.

Jamie responded, allowed his generosity to be drawn out, to admit more than he'd intended. 'Because he loved you. He didn't want to lose what he had. He'd never have left you. He regretted the way he was.'

Brigid took the empty mug off him, and put it on the grass. 'You didn't want to come, did you?'

'No. Dessi made me. Si knew about others before Rupert, you see.'

'I see. Not to the credit of either of them, was it? It's not that I'm against . . . you know . . . Just that he was both. I suppose it was his feminine qualities I loved. They were what made us close. What he loved, you know, was our life together. It was orderly. We thought we had perfection. I was part of the pattern. I understand how he felt, Jamie, because I felt the same.'

'You loved each other.' Jamie smiled wryly at her.

The smile was something to occupy his face, a change of expression to stop his features crumpling.

Brigid recognized the developments of their conversation, like a slow minuet. It was now her turn to respond, to be generous, to admit. 'I loved our *life*. I'm not certain I ever lusted after him. I wouldn't have loved him at all if he hadn't been elegant. I suppose I loved him like a brother. And that's not good enough. If he hadn't found you I'd never have known. I'm amazed I can say this.'

'Poor Rupert.'

'Poor all of us, really. Have *you* discovered anything?'

'Yes. I see what enabled him to live with himself. Why he stayed with you. You created order for him. It's how you are, through and through. I could never do that.'

'You could.'

'No. I'm not what I seem.'

'Rupert must have thought you beautiful. You *are* beautiful, Jamie.' Generosity welled up within Brigid now that she could see so clearly. They'd both been so hurt, and she wanted to stop this vulnerable man from any more pain.

'My name isn't Jamie. It's Leonard. I'm not a playwright. I do *write* plays, but none ever get performed. Actually, I'm a rep for a firm selling pest-control chemicals. Not exactly green either, I'm afraid. Rupert didn't know that.'

Brigid and the youth stared at each other. She tried to take in what he'd said, amazed he'd confessed so much. Brigid saw he was more hurt than she'd ever been, and so vulnerable she was tempted to put her arms round him, cradle and comfort him. Had that golden head rested on her shoulder, it wouldn't have been the scalp of the enemy whose power she could steal, but that of a child whose face was grazed. He was staring, desolated, at the grass.

'You're Jamie to me,' said Brigid and held out her hands. She'd won the day, but there was no need to win. The marriage had proved stronger than the affair. The rival was diminished, a beautiful butterfly turned into a caterpillar.

'We've said everything, haven't we?' Jamie would never be a youth again. Perhaps he'd truly loved Rupert, in a way she never had.

'Why the New Age thing?'

'Started when I was in hell over Rupert dying. Lived near the Morrows. Si seemed quite spiritual at the time. Some sort of answer to it all. I came up here for the solstice because it might be an idea for a play. A musical. You could get some great songs out of it.' He laughed, as if he knew he could never do it.

'Keep writing. You may have something worth telling now. Hold the pain within you and it could become a pearl.'

He hesitated, took her hands briefly in his, and turned away. She watched him get back into his car, with none of the jauntiness of his arrival.

When he'd gone, she sat on the doorstep, for only the second time of her adult life. She put her head on her hands and cried. She cried for the lost dreams of them all, for their deceptions, and for the waste of living it had all been. Their wedding feast, the celebrations of her union with Rupert, so long extended, were finished. Perfection is cold, it gleams and it glitters, but it doesn't glow. That was all her marriage had been, a pursuit of the ultimately impossible. She'd not lived in her marriage, she'd existed in it, and thought she was happy. Poor Rupert. Poor Brigid. Poor Jamie. And poor Aeneas too.

Aeneas walked up to the cottage with Alys. Brigid hadn't told him about it, but Bessie had. 'Looks like Brigid might be staying,' she said. He carried with him another Rowan sapling. He was at the bottom of the path that led up to the gate when Jamie drove by, looking neither to left nor right. Aeneas had to crouch back into the hedge. He recognized him from the day at Bewick Hill. He extricated himself and went on up the path, and saw Brigid sitting on the step, crying. He waited for a minute, but knew he didn't know how to comfort her. Angry with himself, he walked back down to the pub.

Jamie was sitting alone in a corner with a double whisky. 'I'll join you if you don't mind,' said Aeneas going over. 'Same again? I think you know a friend of mine. Brigid.'

Jamie was already slurred. It wasn't his first glass. 'Dear old Brigid. I buggered her husband, you know.'

'Er, what was that you said?' Aeneas spilled at least a fluid ounce down his carefully ironed shirt.

'We were lovers. Got that? I expect you'd got me down as one of *those*.' Jamie flapped his wrist and twisted his voice into contorted Home county vowels, which wasn't especially logical.

'I see.' Aeneas downed what was left in his glass as if it were bitter medicine. He picked up Jamie's glass and fetched them doubles.

'He was a smashing bloke, you know. Lovely. Knowing. Perfectionist, he was, I suppose. God, I miss him still. What do *you* do?'

'Used to teach. I write now.'

'Same here. Plays. The Royal Court's looking one of mine over at the moment actually. Hoping Ken might accept the lead. If he's up to it. It's pretty demanding stuff, you know.'

'So you knew Rupert well?' Aeneas needed to build up a picture of Rupert. He needed to know. Because of Brigid.

'Right on. I knew him well. In the biblical sense.' Jamie sniggered to himself. 'Course, if it's not Ken, there's always Hugh. He's only in films though. Do *you* know by any chance if Hugh does plays?'

'Hugh who?'

'Hugh who. Fantastic. That's really funny. Who Hugh. You're a very witty man, you know that?' Jamie burped appreciatively.

'What about Rupert?'

Jamie frowned. 'Could be bloody annoying. Obsessed with cleanliness. Everything in its place. Little minded, really. That's what he was. Yep. Pernickety. Do you want to know something? I don't understand how that woman put up with him for all those years.'

'She loved him.'

Jamie nodded. He stopped and looked speculative. Whisky was clearing his mind wonderfully. There comes a moment when everything is so simple. So obvious. Pared down to the truth. Nuances lost. Like he'd never realized until a moment ago that Rupert was a damned annoying person. Now he could see into Brigid's mind. If she didn't find him a pain in the neck it was because she liked that life. That was what she wanted, their life, not Rupert.

'She liked their life,' said Jamie. 'I think that was the measure of it.'

'Liked their life. More than him?'

'I bet it was just like that. I think you've hit the nail on the bottom there.'

'She might find someone else.' Aeneas looked down into his glass. 'Someone different.'

'Absolutely. Not like him.'

'Someone who loves her for what she is. For all of her, everything.'

'She won't find him up here. She likes her shopping.' What nice words those were. She and shopping. So easy to say. They proved he was sober. He said them again. 'She and shopping.' He was good at choosing words. 'I'm good at choosing words, you know.'

'I used to think that. That she liked her shopping.'

'I don't know how she put up with him. I really *really* don't. I *really* mean that. Sincerely.'

'Nor do I.' Aeneas tasted the whisky on his tongue, fiery and apparently blended for its harshness. He drained the glass. He never drank spirits. He didn't need whisky. He didn't need alcohol. He'd been told all he ever needed to know.

Jamie leaned across and put a hand on Aeneas's thigh. 'I'm so glad to see you. I'm a playwright, you know. I'm going to give Ken a ring. Have you got his number at all? I expect someone will have. How about we get good and drunk *together*?'

'Some other time,' said Aeneas politely and stood up. He threaded an approximately straight path home.

Brigid went to her car parked beside the gate, and took out the litre can of paint from the boot and a large brush. Soon the whole of the back wall of the main room was covered in gleaming white, crisp as new snow, and the sun shone in through the open front door, reflecting, and filling the whole house with a bright light. As caves and temples in ancient religions are chosen or positioned to reflect the sun at dawn, or at its peak, and become significant in their orientation, so the cottage was significant in reflecting the sun on this day. On this particular afternoon, of all afternoons in August, the white wall shouted back at the world that Brigid was finally healed.

Harvest Moon

Lammas tide is with us, although it is only August. The Celtic year was far more subtly in tune with the turning of the seasons. Today people think of August as summer, they take their holidays then. But in August, there is a cool mist in the early morning, it is the time of harvest, and there are berries on the trees. On your rowan tree in particular, although it is young and newly planted, the berries glow, brick-red, not crimson, in the evening light. They are a comforting colour, not a challenging one.

So wrote Aeneas in an unsent letter. He was meant to be writing his book, his celebration of Celtic thought, but the words he wrote turned into something different. They began to form after his drink with Jamie.

You have come to your third stage, Brigid, another of your triple images of woman. You will become the matron, you are the goddess of midwifery and fostering. You'll be fulfilled, as you've never truly been, and you'll find contentment. It's the nature of woman, it's a miracle such happiness can exist and come forth generation after generation. For a while, there will be no room in your life for anything other. Then you may become a maiden once more.

In the Celtic world the harvest moon is around September 23rd. It is the full moon at the equinox, when the moon rises to a point opposite the sun, and close to the eastern point of the horizon. At this time of the year, the moon is strong at sunset, and the day is prolonged for the gathering of the corn. Even through the night, the moonlight is strong enough to work by. Some years this is welcome, for in September, Herne, the leader of the wild hunt, is heard in the storms. Those who know his nature can sense his coming, and must save their harvest.

How can I know if I'll ever reap my own harvest of content? Brigid was a goddess, and still is. Can you possibly forget the beautiful Rupert? Did Jamie tell you everything? Perhaps if I find a tie to match my shirt? Would it help if I learned to cook?

The Celtic Way, With my love, Aeneas

Brigid rang Perdita frequently. These days she was available, not always out. She sounded tired and listless. 'Why don't you come up here now?' Brigid asked. 'I can spoil you, and you'll be ready if anything starts early.'

'Not yet, Mum, not just yet.'

'Have you bought anything for the baby?'

'Not yet. Don't fuss.'

Brigid went to Berwick and bought a packet of disposable nappies and some baby oil and felt better.

There was a letter from Jan Morrow, who sounded at last as if they were on their way home. 'Here we are in the States. Don't ask me which one, we're dashing through like a dose of salts. Somehow, we missed New Zealand. Just forgot it was there. Philip finished his dolphin poem, and was having a little snooze when it blew away out to sea. We could see it floating on the horizon. He was quite pleased and said it was a spiritual end, but I thought of it as litter and was cross with him. I'm lauded here for my accent. People stare at me. We'll definitely be home by mid-November.'

Perdita came back to Highmoor House in September. The hot weather made her tired and she slept much of the day. It was damp in the mornings, and early evening, but in the middle of the day it was still like summer, ideal weather except for the pregnant.

Reginald overhauled the electric wiring which he said was dodgy. He took up carpets, and the whole house looked dishevelled. He stuck tools into sockets and watched the electricity fizz. 'Pure energy,' he said. 'Magic.' Brigid hoped he wouldn't electrocute himself while only half way through. Magda undertook her summer end ablution. She washed every item of clothing she possessed, all at the same time, and walked round the kitchen stark naked. Sky-clad was too romantic a term to describe Magda's ample and lethargic folds of pulp. Brigid lent her Jan Morrow's dressing-gown, which was blue rayon with orange dragons on it.

Duncan was into jam. There were bowls and pots and saucepans of it all over the kitchen, the floor, the table, the window sills. Wasps hovered and drowned. Duncan sang and was a happy man. He was in an excess of plenitude. Jam asked no questions. He frequently rang his office with a handkerchief over his nose and told them his virus had still not been diagnosed, but not to think the worst.

Sometimes Brigid and Perdita went to the cottage. It was peaceful there and got them away from the commune. They took two wicker sun chairs from the shed at Highmoor House and made them comfortable with pillows. Brigid put them in the shade of the lime tree, which was no longer dropping its sweet stickiness to the ground. She brought out cool drinks, and sat with Perdita in the afternoons, as she dozed. She watched her sleeping child, and was continually surprised that Perdita could be related. She lay, now, ungainly on the pillows, her stomach heaving as she breathed, like some beached dolphin. Her hair was lank and the fabric of her dress was stretched. Brigid was filled with a deep love for her. She was choked with compassion, and with the need to take all pain away, to bear it for her. Brigid wasn't thinking of the pain of childbirth, but what would come with having no man to help with the child. Perdita needed affection and attention. Perdita wasn't an agreeable reflection of herself, not the ideal daughter, but she loved her. She loved her more than if she *had* been a flattering accessory. Perfection was no longer necessary.

Perdita wasn't interested in preparing for the baby's arrival. 'We'll go into Mothercare in Gateshead,' said Brigid. 'We'll go to the Metrocentre. They'll have *everything*.'

Perdita said, 'Do I have to go?'

'Yes,' said Brigid.

In the end Si and Dessi went along as well to advise. It took a long time working out where Mothercare was in the huge shopping mall, but they eventually located it on the upper floor in the blue zone. Brigid bought six of everything and eight packets of disposable nappies, newborn size.

'Seems a long way to come for just these things,' said Dessi. He was right.

'It's part of the ceremonial. Motherhood. Grand-motherhood,' explained Brigid. 'The pleasure of preparation.' She wished Perdita would show more enthusiasm. 'I must go to Asda.'

'I'm not coming,' said Perdita.

'Me neither,' said Si.

Brigid stood in the middle of Asda and breathed a long sigh of contentment. Over there were Cambozola cheese and St Agur. In the opposite direction lay sweet potatoes and yams on the vegetable racks, out of season asparagus and pancetta. Most wondrous of all, on the shelf in front of her was a whole row of bottles of walnut oil. They stood as beacons of a civilization she'd thought lost. There was pesto, oil with herbs in the bottle, and Italian dried mushrooms.

Brigid treated herself to a tour of all the food she hadn't seen for months. She bought little, but felt a better woman, restored, and invigorated from within.

When she got back to where she'd left the others, they'd gone.

The yellow zone of the multicoloured display suggested where they could be. They were children all of them at heart.

Si insisted first on a coffee in the Village Olde Worlde Teashop with a water wheel outside. The room was crowded and they squashed into a corner at the back. The shopping took up two chairs. Perdita wriggled on her chair trying to get comfortable. She closed her eyes and breathed shallow and fast.

'Do you want to talk?' Si asked.

'No.'

'Share it with me. Give. Give out. Feel better about yourself.'

'I'm hot,' said Perdita.

Si shrugged his shoulders and stared moodily into his coffee. 'What am I doing here, in a cathedral to materialism, for heaven's sake?' He glared accusingly at Dessi. 'I should be out there, telling them. Spreading my gospel. Pointing out to the poor sods what a mess they're making of the world. We must move. Next week. Definite.' He sighed. 'It's quite nice in here, isn't it?'

'Sanctioned by the church commissioners,' Dessi pointed out. 'Maybe it was built to get people together. A spirit of community.'

'People gathered ready for me to speak? Should I say something now?'

'They don't look quite ready to me,' said Dessi.

'Hi, there.' Si leaned over to the two women at the next table. One had a tight perm and a firmly-belted pink raincoat. She was about to gouge a lump out of her doughnut. They other woman's grey loo brush style hair was once dyed an alarming shade of carrot, a suggestion of which now lingered only at the ends. There were sacs of navy mascara on her lower lashes, and holly-red lipstick seeped into the crazed lines round her mouth. 'Have you considered,' Si asked, 'the possibility of a collective consciousness?'

'Don't look at him,' hissed the tight perm, out of the side of her mouth. 'If he doesn't go away you can call the management.' She took a determined stab at her doughnut, eyes averted.

The elderly punk ignored the advice, and sat back studying Si. Slowly and deliberately she licked her lips. She stretched out her leg and reached his ankle. She rubbed her foot slowly up and down his shin.

Si shifted his chair so he couldn't see her. What was it with him that made women go for his legs?

'Never fails,' said the matriarchal tart to the tight perm.

'You said people must find their own truth.' Dessi was embarrassed.

'I have to open their eyes.'

'You're the only one who *knows*, are you?'

'I may well be.'

'That's how they all start. Religious leaders.'

'I have to do something with my life.'

'You're a megalomaniac.'

'Stop going on,' said Perdita. 'As if it matters. Think what I've got to go through.'

'You have all my sympathy,' said Si momentarily remembering his love of humanity before sinking back into frustration. 'You reap as you sow, Perdita darlin'. What happened? Some hot night in the back of a car?'

'Watch it, Si,' said Dessi.

'Or is he married?'

'Shut up,' said Perdita, keeping her voice low, 'or you'll regret it.'

'Right. Right. Everyone calm down. Honestly, Perdita, if you want to talk, then talk. But please, please don't sit there glowering. Get a little joy into your life. Feel the throb of what's good, what should be a natural joy for you. Get feeling.' Si smiled his beautiful comforting smile, his magic simple way of putting the world right. He patted her hand as it rested beside her coffee cup. Then smiled again, more intense, more healingful.

'I *am* feeling,' snarled Perdita. 'Why don't you get *thinking*?'

'Thinking?'

'Yep. Thinking.'

'Like what?'

'Like my baby's due on the twenty-fifth of September.'

'Twenty-fifth. Yes. Got that. Fine. So?'

'That will be nine months after it got conceived, right?'

'Right.' Si nodded, and let the calculation filter through to his mind. 'So . . . ?' He sat up straight.

'I'm flattered you remember,' said Perdita.

Dessi went outside. He leaned over the water wheel and looked down into the artificial stream. The lady with the tight perm could see him through the window and wondered if he were about to throw up. He'd wondered where Si had slept on Christmas night. He'd told himself it wasn't possible. Perdita wouldn't have done that. He'd been wrong.

Perdita and Si looked at each other in mutual horror.

'Rubbish,' said Si.

'Even you did biology, I imagine.'

'If it was me, you'd have said before.'

'I didn't mean ever to say.'

'I can't have anything to do with this. I have work to do. I must fulfil my destiny.'

'Fine.'

'You don't mean it, do you?'

Si closed his eyes for a full minute. Only through meditation could he detach himself from the trivialities of the material world. None of which mattered. He felt the breath which is life itself ebb and flow within him. He'd never been more centred in a meditation. The world dropped from his shoulders. He was free. He was uncluttered. Perdita was not to impinge upon him. He opened his eyes, stood up and said, as if nothing had happened, 'We might as well enjoy ourselves till Brigid turns up. Follow me.'

* * *

Brigid was right. They'd gone to Metroland. A place of magic. Brigid watched the galleon sway up and up, then swing over as if it were riding the ocean. The children were screaming with pleasure. She moved out of the way to let the trainload of toddlers snake round at floor level. On the roundabout the seats swung out over the people's heads. Suddenly there was a huge whoosh above her, and the galaxy roller coaster thundered along under the roof, passengers screaming. As the express curved to the left Brigid saw Si with his arms in the air, face contorted with the thrill. Behind him Perdita clutched the rail, white with fear. Dessi, behind her, looked grim and was clutching a large carrier of nappies.

Brigid spotted where the roller coaster would finish and ran over. As she helped her off, Perdita nearly fainted. They got her to a bench.

'Are you mad?' Brigid said to Si. 'Breathe deeply, Perdita.'

'She's a free woman,' said Si. 'You know that was bloody marvellous. A fantastic sensation. Transportive. Anyone coming again?'

'We're going straight home,' said Brigid. 'There's no knowing what might happen to Perdita now.'

Si ignored her and strode to the roller coaster. 'Only takes four minutes,' he shouted over his shoulder.

'Leave him.' Brigid was tart. 'He can make his own way home.'

Dessi watched Si flying ecstatically round the roof. Si was in shock. He was out of control. He needed Dessi's loyalty more than ever. Perdita was white and shaken on the bench. Perdita needed him now. She needed his protection. With a guilty glance up at the roller coaster, he took Perdita's arm, and followed Brigid to the car park.

'Look,' said Dessi, when they approached the car, 'there's . . .'

'It's not,' interrupted Brigid. 'It's wearing a collar.'

Si couldn't believe Brigid had left without him. Where was Dessi, for heaven's sake? Dessi was meant to look after him. Care for him. Look after the practical side of his life. He only fully accepted the unfaithfulness of them both when he realized the car had gone from the car park. He'd no money on him, so couldn't get a bus. He wandered out of the Metrocentre with the idea of hitching a lift. Now his hair had grown again he looked fairly respectable. While he was jerking his thumb meaningfully towards home he suddenly saw it.

Actually he saw two things and wasn't certain which came first. Tara, his totem beast, was poised on the pavement, tail in the air, ready to leap. Above her was the gleaming Ducati with no security locks. The cat leapt and landed delicately on the saddle. She sat, turned and looked back towards Si. Around her neck glowed a golden collar. Si could see it was a torc, the necklet of the aristocratic Celt, the mark of the noble spirit. When he fully registered what he saw, Tara jumped from the saddle and paced herself away, tail erect. She didn't glance back. No need, thought Si.

He couldn't believe at first that the bike was waiting for him. Strange how life gave you what you needed at exactly the right moment. Like the ass waiting for Jesus. It happened to men of destiny. The bike turning up, confirmed his karma.

He sat astride it. He revved it up. How sweet the sound.

'Follow me,' he said to anyone who might be around. 'I am the leader.'

He roared away, up the street, overtaking cars on the inside, weaving through the mundane Fords and Vauxhalls, a man who was alive to all the possibilities, a man whom no one could now stop from fulfilling his mission. The One whom soon all would recognize. He was to be a father, yet he must not be confined. It was more urgent than ever he fulfilled his destiny, that domestication shouldn't impede him on his path.

Si had ridden motor bikes before, but never one like this, including the Ducati he'd once owned. Never one where the power was alive to so light a touch. He took the country roads to avoid the police, though he was surely immune to such a banality. The wind tugged his hair behind him, flowing free from his head, like a child's picture of the rays of the sun. He'd never cut it since the miraculous healing.

At last, he could feel the power. The power of the wind, the speed of the bike, and his own indomitable coming to his apogee. The curves in the lane were exciting, he never knew what was coming next. Faster. Faster. What would he say to them, when he confronted the powers that would resist him? He didn't need to think about that. The words would be given him. He was in touch with the creative power of the earth, in contact with the great imagination. He could do anything. He would do great things. His parents would bow down before him. His school masters would remember him with wonder, and quake at their old ignorance. The one collective consciousness was carrying him on. It was an act of worship, a celebration of the element of air. His was the glory. His was the power. His was the elevation of the human spirit to total divinity. He would sacrifice his life unto this end.

Unfortunately, a Ducati, while being a fine piece of engineering, is not particularly responsive to spiritual forces. Nor is it independently intelligent. It needs to be steered. The lane went sharp right, and neither the bike nor Si went with it.

Aeneas drove home slowly from Berwick. The year had turned, and the trees, though yet green, were beginning to shed some leaves. They drifted in front of the windscreen, small hints of an imminent death. Soon would come the beauty of red and gold, the apricot of the maples, colours to warm the eye against the coming frosts.

He'd bought a wok in the smart kitchen boutique. It had been an adventurous thing to do, he knew. The sales girl there, all mascara and shiny red mouth had assured him that she and her boyfriend used theirs all the time and it was ever so easy. Aeneas presumed they were talking about the same thing, and asked how long it took. That depended, she said, on what they were doing.

As he drove he wondered what he should do next. Should he use the wok tonight, and then slip out casually that the green beans and tomatoes had come out a treat in the stir fry. Or should he plead total ignorance and ask Brigid to show him how to use it. He'd bought chicken joints in case that was the decision he finally took.

He decided as the afternoon was so bright and fresh that he would take the lanes to the village and keep off the main road. He could drive slowly with the windows wound down and take pleasure in the journey.

He was five minutes into the drive among the rolling hills, sometimes passing a solitary cottage garden in its last blooming of lavender and sedums, when he came across the motor bike lying at the side of the lane. He almost didn't stop because he thought it was abandoned. Only when he was almost past did he see the body lying beyond it in the hedge.

Aeneas made himself get out of the car. He was frightened by death and blood and possible nasty sights. He went across the lane and turned his head sideways to look at the half-buried face.

He looked down on a frighteningly still Si and tried to see if he were breathing. He felt the forehead, which was warm. He dug under the body and located the wrist. Yes, there was a pulse. He was alive at least.

He daren't move him and risk further injury. Few cars came this way. If only he were a modern person he would have a mobile phone. Aeneas covered Si with the rug that protected the car against Alys when she was muddy. It was muddy itself and hairy but would keep him warm. He put a warning red triangle up, just before the motor bike and drove back to the last cottage in search of a phone.

The ambulance was quick and arrived as Aeneas got back to Si. His breathing was slower and Si looked paler.

'What happened?' The man spoke as they established whether it was safe to move him.

'I don't know. I found him like this.'

'You're saying you weren't involved? The police will want to know. They'll be along in a minute themselves.' Instinctively the ambulance man noted the number of his car.

'I'll come with you to the hospital. I recognize him.'

'That's helpful. Can you inform the relatives?'

'His family is abroad, but I can tell the people where he lives.'

Si showed no sign of regaining consciousness. 'Was he new to the bike, sir, do you know?'

'I think he must have been.'

Aeneas waited for two hours in casualty, while doctors and nurses came and went. There were X-rays, and finally Si was wheeled away to a reception ward. 'You can see him now,' said a nurse, who looked tired, and whose wide generous mouth had collapsed with her into harassed vexation.

Si was lying in the bed, as if laid out. His breathing was so shallow it was scarcely visible. His skin had a creamy waxiness about it that wasn't reassuring. The nurse put his arms outside the bedclothes, straight down by his side. His head and shoulders were propped up so he wouldn't choke. He looked wonderfully untroubled, as if the world were nothing to do with him.

'Is he all right?' Aeneas whispered when a nurse came with paperwork on clip boards to festoon over the bedhead.

'Concussion,' she said. 'Brain scan tomorrow if there's no improvement.'

'Does he need anything?'

'He might if he wakes up. Toiletries. Pyjamas. Even if he seems fine tomorrow he'll need observation.'

'He'll be all right, though?'

'Wasn't wearing a helmet, was he?' She had little sympathy for fools.

'I'll take you to see him tomorrow,' said Aeneas.

'There's no point in going this evening.' Brigid couldn't leave Perdita, beached on the sofa looking apprehensive.

'Oh dear,' wailed Magda. 'What's it all coming to?'

'What was he doing on a motor bike?' Brigid asked.

'Getting home,' said Dessi. 'I should never have left him.'

'He must have nicked it,' said Brigid. 'There'll be the police.'

'I can't leave him lying there,' said Dessi. 'What if he comes round?'

'Take some toothpaste,' said Brigid tartly. She added to Aeneas, 'You'd better have something to eat.'

'I've got a wok. I bought it. We could use that.' He watched her face, looking for her reaction. He fetched the box from the car and tore it open like an excited child. 'Look. Recipes. Chopsticks. Four little bowls. You get all that as well. What are they for?'

'I've done us all duck in plum conserve,' said Duncan. 'There's a surfeit.'

'I've got some chicken.' Aeneas was not to be side-tracked.

'That's a lovely idea, Aeneas. I think you should use the wok. Perdita likes chicken too,' said Brigid. She wanted to be away from the followers tonight. She'd given too much of herself to them.

'Suit yourselves,' said Duncan.

Brigid sat at the kitchen table and watched Aeneas searching through the instructions, sometimes turning back, frowning slightly. He was so different to Rupert, who'd have made a witty, elegant show of the process, had his spices and herbs at the ready, mastered the technique in moments.

'What the hell's a wonton?' Aeneas asked. He closed

his eyes as he threw beans and onions into the hot oil. He winced when the oil spat onto his hand. He put so much energy into his cooking his shirt was flapping loose and untidy. He stared at the joints of chicken with woolly and impractical curiosity. He could never be elegant. From time to time he glanced at Brigid to see if she were impressed. 'I hope I'm doing this right.'

She thought, you don't need to do it right. You don't need to change.

Some time later they sat down to eat. 'What do you think?'

'Fine,' said Brigid, 'for a first attempt.'

'Burnt food is carcinogenic,' said Perdita. 'Honestly, Aeneas, with the baby and all, do you mind me asking Duncan if there's any duck left over?'

'Perhaps five minutes less next time, do you think?'

'Less time and more stirring,' said Brigid, 'but it's edible.'

'I'm not that hungry, actually. With Si and everything.'

'Me neither. Bit anxious about Perdita.'

Dessi took the van to the hospital and had trouble parking it. He found a spot so far away that he lost the hospital. Eventually he got himself to the desk in the entrance lobby. The girl, who was blonde and spotty, said it was definitely ward seven. He got the impression she couldn't read very well. Ward seven was at the far end of the hospital, as situations always were for Dessi. His footsteps echoed on the polished floor, and he tried to walk quietly. He didn't like hospitals and he wondered if Si would look different, in which case Dessi might throw up. Still, they'd be used to that in a hospital.

As Si wasn't a grape person Dessi had had the presence of mind to grab the bottle of vodka and had wrapped it discreetly in a Somerfields bag. He might need it to steady himself if there were much blood. He couldn't let himself think Si might even be dead. Aeneas said he was unconscious when he left him. Unconscious is a long way from being dead. Usually.

The main ward was long, but there was a variety of small rooms off the ward corridor. Dessi located Si from a list above the duty desk. *S. Morrow* it said in childish writing. Room 3. From doorways came the smell of urine, disinfectant and burning. There were no nurses about. The other patients either slept or stared at him with accusing eyes. Si wasn't in either of the beds next to the door which Dessi took as a sign death wasn't imminent. He moved cautiously into the room. The third patient was heavily bandaged but the state of the toenails indicated this wasn't Si either. They were yellow and curling, they were snail nails of the elderly and unkempt. Curtains were drawn round the fourth bed.

He was unsure what to do. This had to be Si's bed. Was he so ill he needed the privacy? 'Si?' Dessi called softly.

There was no answer. It would be embarrassing if he pulled the curtains aside and Si were balanced on a bedpan.

A swishing sound came from behind the curtain.

'Si?'

No reply and no sign of any staff, no ministering angels around the beds of the sick. Dessi stepped forward, flicked the curtain aside as if by mistake, and took a lightning fast glimpse of the bed.

It was empty. On the floor lay a heap of crumpled

sheets. By the bed stood a nurse, stripping the mattress. She was pretty with a pre-Raphaelite nose, rosebud mouth and blond bob. 'He's gone,' she said, as the curtain fell back.

Dessi stared at the curtain, still seeing the empty bed. His stomach felt as if it was upended, and he knew even vodka could do no good. Slowly he walked out of the ward, and found his way to the street. He leaned up against a wall, staring into space. What would he ever do without Si. Si had sustained him through all of his childhood and then his youth. It would not be too much to say he loved Si. Only in the purest way. There was nothing physical in it, only a delight in his company, and faith in his decisions. Now Si was gone. He wondered if he should go to the mortuary. He decided he couldn't bear to see Si lying dead. Not anybody really, but certainly not Si.

The worse thing was being disillusioned with Si and having no chance to talk it over properly. Perhaps there was a goddess. He would never forgive himself for abandoning him in Metroland. None of it was Si's fault. It was all his.

'What's up with you?' A vaguely familiar voice accosted him. Dessi looked up from the brick wall and saw the vicar. 'I've come to visit Mrs Moulden. Strangulated hernia.'

'He's dead,' said Dessi.

'Dead?'

'Si.'

'Dearest Lord. Poor chap. What happened?'

'Road accident.'

'God rest his soul. Now why don't you hang about here while I visit the old broiler and I'll run you home.'

'I've got the van.'

'As you wish.' Cedric scuttled into the hospital. He wondered if he could make use of Si for a sermon.

Dessi never knew how he drove home, lucky not to have an accident. With cold air blowing on his face he began to think more clearly. He knew what to do. Tomorrow he would buy candles. Perhaps he could find some in the house. Somehow, in his mind, he knew he must perform some sort of service for Si tonight, something independent of any formal dismissing there might be later. Later, of course, he would have to prevent Cedric from taking over the burial. That was another problem. He would light candles in Si's room, and burn them through the night. They would symbolize the spirit, allow him to leave his space on earth in peace. They'd never discussed this but Dessi knew Si would approve of candles. A candlelight vigil. Si would like a vigil. It was his sort of thing. It was what Dessi must do.

As the night came, the rain began. At first it was a steady beat, but within half an hour it was torrential, beating against the house with vicious intensity. Ten minutes later Perdita yelped. 'I felt it,' she shouted. 'As if my back was being all squeezed up. I can't stand much of this.'

'It could be the start. Just keep calm.' Brigid thought it looked like a long night, especially if there was this much fuss at the very first twinge. 'Sit at the table,' she suggested, 'and lean your arms on it. It's supposed to help.' She wished Aeneas hadn't gone home. He said Perdita needed an early night, but she suspected he'd gone to get himself a sandwich.

'Oh God,' said Perdita.

Dessi came into the kitchen, wet from the short walk from the car, and looking worse than Perdita.

'What's up with you?'

'I don't think I should tell you now.' Dessi sensed this was not the time for Perdita to hear.

'Is he still out?'

Dessi said nothing, and poured himself a glass of water.

'*Dessi*! Has something happened?'

He jerked his head to fetch Brigid over to the sink, so Perdita wouldn't hear. 'Si's dead.'

Brigid sat down at the table. 'If only I'd waited for him,' she whispered. 'Why was I so angry? How could I be so stupid? I'm sorry.' She got up and put her arms round Dessi.

'It wasn't you. It was him. It was me. I was his friend. He never was reasonable.'

'Is Si OK?' Perdita called between moans.

'I expect so,' said Brigid, trying to keep her voice level.

Dessi found all the candles he could, and put them in holders and milk bottles in Si's bedroom. He sat cross-legged on the floor, facing the bed, closed his eyes, and tried to feel the universal soul of which Si was now a part.

He didn't make it. Now that he'd got his mind together he wasn't certain he had a soul. He'd been right the evening of the beach barbie. You couldn't ever know. Si couldn't know. Si had *decided* too much. He blew out the candles and sat in the dark. He thought about Perdita.

Reginald checked his wiring. It was a bigger task than he'd expected. The conduits were a maze, and he wasn't certain he'd identified all the paths. He decided that night he would sleep in the van, it might be safer.

Duncan sulked because no-one ate his duck. A wok is not a sophisticated way to cook, it's for Chinese peasants. And the smells got up one's sleeves.

From the start Perdita was not a good patient. She writhed and screamed at every early spasm. She was lucky to progress fast. The contractions increased in frequency and got stronger. Magda floated into the kitchen, strewing sprigs of marjoram. 'My mind is so clear tonight,' she said. 'I want to hear the first cries of the child. My life will change from that hour.'

'You need an early night,' said Brigid, and firmly pushed her towards the door. 'To be fresh for the change in direction.'

'Bless you all,' said Magda. 'I look forward to it.'

Cedric drove slowly in the rain, the wipers on double speed, and he could still scarcely see more than a foot in front. Mrs Moulden had been a right pain. She discussed her funeral plans even though she was coming out in two days' time. He was later than he meant to be. Ahead of him, a figure staggered out from the kerb, buffeted by the gale. He ought to give a person out in this weather a lift. You never knew these days. They'd murder you anywhere. Heaven may have been Cedric's ultimate destination and his faith in it absolute, but he was not ready to go there yet. He drove slowly, staring out into the sheet of water that distorted everything beyond it.

He could see now that the figure was a man, but weird. He wore a white gown which blew like a cloud when the wind blustered one way, then draped soggily like a wet sail draping a mast as it blew the other. He wasn't steady on his feet and was buffeted by the wind.

As Cedric drew alongside, the man turned and peered into the car. Cedric wound the window down to see more clearly.

'Christ.' Cedric stared at the gaunt and tortured face.

'It's me.' Si held out his hands for help, as if to display his stigmata. The faint voice confirmed for Cedric this was indeed a ghost.

Cedric's faith was founded on certain knowledge of the Resurrection, a belief that had never been shaken, never questioned. He couldn't accept what his eyes told him. There could never be a second such rising, and certainly not of a person like Si. As Cedric stared at the drenched man, he remembered Si had walked . . . oh no . . . remembered Si had walked on the sea. The foundations of his faith were rocking like a loose tooth in its socket. Cedric put his foot down and drove recklessly on into the night.

'I'll ring the ambulance,' said Brigid at midnight. 'I can't drive *and* look after you. Give ourselves plenty of time. Anyway, they'll give you something to help the pain.'

The torrential rain drummed mockingly against the windows as she heard the ambulance official on the phone. 'The road to your village is flooded. The rain's coming down faster than the drains can carry it away. Is this an emergency? If so, you should contact your GP. Is he in the village? You could ring us later and the water may have subsided.'

Doctor Withers sounded annoyed to be woken and told Brigid to let him know when the spasms got to three minutes. It would take him five minutes to walk up.

Brigid sat down at the table opposite Perdita and

stretched out her hands to her daughter. 'Think about breathing out slowly, and letting yourself relax,' she said. 'See this as something wonderful about to happen.' She used the power of her will to try to calm Perdita. She thought of Si and what he would say. His healing hands would have helped now. Don't think about Si, Brigid told herself. Think only of Perdita.

Dessi came down from Si's room more composed. 'I'll get hot water,' he said.

'What for?'

'*I* don't know. But it's what they do in books. I think you put newspaper on the floor. Shoelaces. They use shoelaces to tie the cord.'

'Dessi, this is *not* an emergency. Dr Withers will be here to cope with everything.'

'Si's dead, isn't he? I know he is.' Perdita stared at Dessi, her eyes wide with fear. 'I'm going to die too.'

Aeneas threw open the kitchen door, dripping rain everywhere. 'The road's flooded. I'm here in case you need anything.'

'Aeneas,' said Brigid and touched his arm gratefully. 'It's like the cavalry's arrived.'

Brigid rang Dr Withers at three-thirty, when the pace hotted up and Perdita was going wild. He was a desiccated man, not made gentle and kindly by his association with the rural life and the sick. His upper lip was a perpetual sneer. Pyjama legs showed beneath his trousers, and he had that smell about him suggesting bedclothes weren't changed often enough. Brigid had seen Mrs Withers in the village, although she'd never spoken. She'd given the impression by the state of her cardigan that she wasn't a woman addicted to her washing machine.

He hustled Perdita to bed, and gave her an injection that she was determined not to admit to be of benefit. 'Be grateful it's all going quick. You're ready to bear down.' There was no consolation in his words.

Brigid wiped Perdita's forehead and smiled encouragingly, feeling *she* was making all the effort.

'Pity there's no father at the head end,' said Dr Withers. 'A law unto themselves, some of you girls today. You've got the hard work to do now, young woman. Give me your full co-operation, if we're to get some sleep before morning.'

Brigid held Perdita's hand, and repeated Dr Wither's instructions. 'Try to push with the next one. Just one good one. It'll soon be over.'

Perdita wailed. 'Shut up, my dear,' said Dr Withers. 'It's misplaced energy. Give your mind over to a good shove.'

'Push, darling. It'll soon be over. Puuush.'

While Brigid mentally pushed, and Perdita writhed, the baby made progress on its own.

Through the window the lightning flashed and forked, a triple showing. There was a crash overhead and the lights went out. It was either the storm or Reginald's tampering.

'Bugger,' said the doctor.

Brigid felt her way to the door. 'Aeneas,' she shouted.

'You stay there. I know where there are candles,' shouted Aeneas. 'I've seen them in the cupboard under the sink.'

A moment later he came upstairs with one lit and carrying two more. 'That's all I could find.' He reached out to find Brigid as she stood at the door. He took her hand to hold as he gave one to her. 'You need only call,' he said. Momentarily he held her arm. The candles flickered, and illuminated the lower part of his face.

There was another strike of lightning. Through the landing window Brigid saw the Rowan-tree shine for one brief moment like silver. Its frail and immature trunk bent with the gale and wasn't broken.

She smiled at Aeneas in the faint light. He was more alive than anyone she knew. She wanted Aeneas to touch her, to love her. There was nothing remotely spiritual in what she felt about Aeneas. Nothing about him was perfect, he was just superbly whole. He lit the second candle from the first.

Dessi shouted, 'There are some more in Si's room. I'll get them for you. Is Perdy OK?' The name sounded odd to Brigid. It reminded her of Joanna Lumley, and anything less like Purdy than Perdita spread-eagled on her bed, being totally uncool, was difficult to imagine.

In the darkness the front door banged.

Aeneas turned, and the two candles lit up the rest of the landing.

At the top of the stairs stood Si wearing a dripping white hospital gown.

He looked aloof and insubstantial in the flickering yellow light.

Perdita could see across the landing from her bed. She screamed. 'It's a dead ghost,' she yelled and screwed her eyes shut.

Dessi moved unbelieving towards him.

'Don't touch me,' said Si.

'They said you were dead,' said Dessi.

'Maybe I am.' There was a wary expression in his eyes, scheming.

'Tell me, Si. You've got to tell me.'

'A resurrection?' Aeneas asked sarcastically.

Si moved smoothly across the floor, gliding, his eyes staring ahead. 'I have experienced what others have not.'

'Si,' said Dessi. 'Tell me what's happened.' He followed him, not daring to get too close.

Perdita opened her eyes and looked across the landing. She saw then it was Si, not a ghost at all. It was the father of her child come to be with her. Yet he would never be with her. It was a single moment, a blink of time's eyelid, when fleetingly everything was as it should be. But as it never would be.

Si looked at Perdita through the open door. He was apart from what was going on in that room. There was nothing between the two of them but a drunken night of sex nine months ago. He felt pity for the feisty girl who'd been so full of life, so exuberant and was now slumped on the bed as if a sacrifice to him. Compassion overwhelmed him, a compassion that was part of the nature of the earth, and he channelled it all towards Perdita. It was the only thing he could do. He stared at her in silence, his eyes vibrant in the candlelight. He felt helpless. Brigid was right. He wasn't a conduit, he was a drain.

Perdita closed her eyes, unable to face the intensity of Si's eyes.

'Leave me now,' said Si to Dessi and Aeneas and leaned on the sill of the landing window.

Perdita opened her eyes and Si was no longer there. 'Bloody hell,' she said, 'let's get on with it. Come on, Doctor. We've got to get my baby born. Don't just sit there.'

The phone rang. Aeneas went warily downstairs with one candle. Tara came up, passing him haughtily with a mouse in her jaws.

'We saw a cat just like Tara in the car park,' said Dessi, for something to say. 'I thought it was her, but we saw she had on a collar. A yellow one.'

'You saw Tara in the car park?' Si's voice was flat.

'No, Si. We saw a cat *like* Tara, but it wasn't Tara.'

'No,' said Si. 'I doubt it was Tara.'

'The hospital,' said Aeneas coming back. 'They might have told us earlier you discharged yourself, Si. Quite comforting. We have the real Si. Not the resurrected version after all.'

'It can't all go wrong now,' said Si and sat on the top stair. 'I'm a healer. Look at my hair. Think how it was.'

Duncan put his head out of the bedroom. 'Less noise, please,' he said and slammed the door shut.

'Did you know,' Aeneas said, 'there are two types of alopecia? I think you had the *areata* variety, that's just hair loss in patches. It seems your patches joined up quite alarmingly. But the condition recovers. With *alopecia totalis*, eyelashes and brows go too. Yours didn't.'

'I do have remarkable eyelashes,' said Si. 'Sod it.' He put his head on his arms.

'You don't care how much trouble you cause, do you?' Aeneas said.

'I was so certain.'

'Always a mistake.'

'What am I going to do?'

'You're going to ask Brigid.'

Dessi brought the rest of the candles. 'Are you *sure* she's OK?'

'Everything's fine.'

Magda drifted across the landing. 'The child cries within. Soon . . . Soon.'

Dessi put her back in her room and wedged a chair

under the handle outside to keep her that way. He went downstairs and found the newspaper Reginald always bought. By the light of one candle he went down the columns.

Candlelight transformed the bedroom. It gave peace. It gave a new dimension. Even Perdita was calm. It didn't, however, affect Dr Withers especially, except to make him scowl more, as he peered down at Perdita.

Brigid held her hand. 'It's going to be fine.'

'Si didn't die.'

'No.'

The flames fluttered and breathed living energy that was a part of the natural world, part of the fire that warmed humankind, and a symbol of the life force itself. Aeneas brought tea for Brigid and Doctor Withers, and barley water for Perdita.

The candles measured the turning of the hours of the night.

Towards daybreak Dr Withers said, 'It's a darned female.' He wrapped the baby in a cot sheet, and handed her over. 'You're supposed to bond with it now, or some such nonsense.' He waited until the afterbirth sloshed out, gathered it up in a plastic bag, washed his hands and left. 'The midwife might get here in the morning, if you're lucky.'

'I could get him struck off for negligence,' said Perdita, but her voice was only joking, and she turned to the baby. She held the child for a long time, gazing down at the small miracle she'd wrought, almost all by herself.

'Try a little suck,' suggested Brigid. Perdita might not take to nurturing. 'Just a little go.' They encouraged the child to find the nipple, to search blindly for her link with life.

'What will you call her?'

'Xanthe.' Perdita touched the child's forehead with her lips, baptizing her by the kiss with which her name began.

'Aeneas,' called Brigid, 'would you like to see the baby?'

He came in looking shy. He looked at the scrap in Perdita's arms, and Brigid could see the pain in his eyes for what he'd never had. He smiled and touched Xanthe's cheek with the back of his fingers. Brigid was staring down at her grandchild and almost purring. He was outside the understanding of Brigid now, for she was the mother, the midwife, the enabler. He must wait.

'I'm glad you saw her first,' she said.

Brigid sat by the window until dawn as Perdita slept, exhausted. She held the child in her arms, tranquil in harmony with herself. She sensed the earth's turning, its balance and plenitude. Her child, and her child's child, and so it would go on, the flame of life passed from one to another. She wouldn't resent growing old, she'd be happy, part of the circle of life, of creation and fertility. The three of them were one with the great creative power of the earth, with the nurturing Gaia. Brigid no longer felt an individual, but that she was of the consciousness that is one. She looked out of the window as the sky grew light, and thought she could smell the misty dawn air, as yet unbreathed.

Xanthe slept, sometimes so lightly that her eyes fluttered under their puffy lids, sometimes so deeply that her breathing was scarcely apparent. Brigid looked at the folds under each eye, and at the snub nose, pushed back to be able to breathe and feed at the same time. She leaned down and smelled the smell that all babies have, which is nothing to do with sick or baby lotion or milk, but only to do with being a baby.

Dessi made them breakfast. He brought it on a tray with a Japanese anemone floating in a spare sugar bowl beside the coffee. He didn't come to see the baby after she was born. He sensed there was no place for him. On Xanthe's first day he looked down into the Moses basket, dazed by the miracle of her.

Brigid dealt with Si. He ate three bowls of cereal.

'I'll do you some eggs,' said Brigid. 'Poached.'

'I fancy some bacon,' Si said. 'No-one can be a vegetarian for ever.'

'Right,' said Brigid.

Dessi passed through the kitchen. 'I'll stock up on disposables,' he said. 'We don't want any rashes.'

Si made the bacon into a butty, and wiped away the fat that ran down his chin with the back of his hand. Then he sat with his hands round his coffee cup, staring morosely out into the garden. 'What am I going to do?'

'With your life?'

'I thought I was different.'

'No-one's as different as you thought you were.'

'I woke up in the evening. I couldn't stand that ward. Terrible smell of pee. It was the old boy opposite. He was moaning all the time. I left. Just walked out. Left my clothes in the locker. Didn't feel up to explaining. I'll wait till the police business is sorted out, then I'll go.'

Brigid sat down opposite Si and took his hands. He'd been a fool. He'd chased his vainglory. But she was grateful to him. He'd changed the way she thought. She was the better for knowing him. 'You could go to India.'

'I'd have to be vegetarian again,' he said, 'just when I'm back on bacon.' Idly, he doodled on the edge of yesterday's newspaper. He drew himself, slumped over the table. There was despair in every line.

'That's it,' said Brigid. 'That's what you must do. Art school.'

'You think?'

'Yes. Yes. Yes. Aeneas will know how to apply and all that.'

'It's what I wanted.'

'You'd be a mature student. Not reliant on your parents.'

'It's you who's my spirit guide. Of course, Brigid is the goddess of inspiration. Yes. I should have known. You're my muse.'

'Shut up, Si. That's over with.'

'Right.'

The followers knew it was over. Reginald made certain his Elsan was empty before the van rumbled away across the gravel. Duncan, in flowered Bermuda shorts and a panama anchored to his head with a wisp of magenta chiffon, disappeared on his motor bike standing upright on the pedals and swinging one arm merrily round like a spasmodic windmill as he went down the lane.

Magda left as she'd arrived, with music. She was thumbing a lift on the A1 when the police picked her up, suspicious of her appearance. They got an emergency call, and whisked Magda through Northumbria to the boisterous sound of their siren. Magda lay back against the seat, rejoicing in her power.

Si stood at the foot of the bed and looked at Perdita. 'I don't know what to say. I could get a job. Get some money for you. I'm sorry. I'm really sorry about this mess.'

'It's not a mess. Anyway, I couldn't have done it without you.'

'Obviously not.'

'I mean the birth. Getting Xanthe born. It was when I saw you there, staring. Something happened to me. I was strong.'

'It wasn't me. I'd have thought it was. Once.'

'It was, Si.'

'My last miracle then.'

Perdita nodded.

'Do you want me to marry you?'

'I don't want anything of you, Si. Only for you to look at her. I want her father to have loved her when he saw her. Even if it's only once.'

Si reluctantly looked at Xanthe who, although sleeping, moved one hand in the air, practising being a person.

'I'm not good enough to cope with this,' he said.

'I'm not asking you to, Si.'

'If Hilly hadn't brought that fruit wine on Christmas day . . . It was a witch's brew.'

'Hilly's spell. It was a blessing.'

A year and a day

Aeneas took the paper from his typewriter and put it with the pile on the floor beside him. The sheets were so white, the letters so mechanical. At last it had come to him. It had come to him standing beside Brigid looking at the baby. It had come when Brigid had touched his arm. Brigid, the mother of memory and the muse of poets. He found his viewpoint. Waterwings was a suitable metaphor.

Highmoor House changed its character. No longer a commune, it became quiet and much tidier. There was no wet washing in the kitchen, or more than one person cooking at the same time. Brigid was glad to see the back of Reginald and Magda, though she missed Duncan's wistful presence with his chopping board and onions.

Most of all she missed Si. She forgot he was lazy and unhinged. She forgot he was irresponsible and the father of Perdita's child. She remembered his calming presence, his smile and the intensity in his eyes. He'd deceived himself about his powers, but he was perceptive. She wondered how he was faring at the art school in Leeds, where Aeneas used his contacts to get him on a course after term started.

Aeneas came to the house once, bringing a present. It was a rattle in a box with multiple assurances of its safety. He was politely enthusiastic about Xanthe's perfections, which were the same as any baby's. He stayed no longer than he need. He said he was working hard on his book.

October came and, although it was still bright, the days became colder. Sweaters appeared, and cardigans for some. Brigid was buying washing powder when Bessie said, her eyes as watchful as ever, 'Poor Aeneas.'

'Why *poor* Aeneas?'

'Hilly must still be hounding him.'

'What do you mean?' Brigid stared at the yellowing pastries on the counter, exposed to the dust of the shop. A dying blue fly was crawling over one of the tarts. Had she been wrong all along, and Aeneas did love Hilly?

'Jealous cow. Always meant to have him, you know. Tricked him into marrying her.'

'She must have been attractive when she was young.'

'She was *easy*.' From the way Bessie spat out the word, Brigid knew Bessie'd fancied Aeneas too. 'Then she tied him to her with guilt. Blamed him for there being no baby. He felt guilty. He got to seem dull. She held onto his feet. Didn't let him swim. He couldn't fulfil himself. He was never free.'

'*He* must have been attractive.' Brigid looked questioningly at Bessie. For the first time since she'd come here, the two understood each other.

'Yes.' She paused. 'I *wasn't* easy. Too proud. Guided by my mother. A very upright lady, her.'

'And now?'

Bessie smiled, her taut, alert features collapsing into resignation. 'People change. I've changed. All I want now is a gossip in the day and the telly at night. But, of course . . .'

'Yes?'

'There's still time for Aeneas. There's time now.' Bessie put one small wrinkled hand over the counter and touched Brigid's arm, soft but firm, like the brush of a bird's wing.

'Would you tell him something from me, Bessie?'

'I would.'

'Tell him *a year and a day*.'

'What are you doing?' Perdita walked round the kitchen winding Xanthe against her shoulder. The baby was always frantic for her milk, frantic for life as Perdita had been. Consequently she swallowed air.

'Making a picnic.'

The stock for the soup was superb, sitting in the bottom of the range oven all night. Parsnips softened in it with parsley and stilton cheese. Its texture was velvet. She made bread dough with soda instead of yeast. Something quick.

Perdita said, 'Are you pleased Dessi's got a job? It's quite a good job, considering he's got no qualifications. He did well at the interview.'

'Yes, I'm pleased. A part of his life is over now. Alnwick is attractive. He'll get to be like everyone else.'

'I don't think he's like *anyone* else.'

'He needs to get away from Si.'

'Mum, Dessi wants me to go with him. He wants to look after me.'

'Oh.'

'I *really* like him.'

'Oh.'

'You don't mind me *not* living in the cottage?'

'It'll be my bolthole. The Morrows are back next week. I don't think I could live in London for ever.'

'I thought Si was resurrected, you know. Just for a minute. From where I was lying the window lit up with lightning and it looked as if there was light and energy actually coming out of Si. It was weird.'

'Si *is* weird. Full stop.' She baked soda bread in the range and wrapped a piece of Redesdale cheese in foil.

Aeneas came round an hour later. He stood on the doorstep, one eyebrow raised. 'Doing anything today?' He looked confident, a man who knew where he was going. 'The child's leaving,' Bessie'd said. 'And to tell you *a year and a day*.'

Aeneas wore a new shirt under the old waxed coat, and a tie of approximately the same colour. Both were blue and they clashed. His hair was cut, not much shorter, but less stuck out at wild angles from his bony head.

'We're going for a picnic,' said Brigid.

Aeneas laughed, and took both her hands in his. He leaned towards her, and seemed to change his mind. 'I'm taking you to Inner Farne. The other island you must see if you're to know yourself. It's important the weather's good enough for us to get over to the island today. John at Seahouses will take us in his fishing boat. He's a friend. The trips all finished at the end of September, thank goodness, and most of the wardens have left too. A couple or so stay on to monitor the seal breeding.'

'Will it really be calm? It's windy.'

'Trust me. Well, trust John. He knows the sea. He says we can make it to the islands.'

This time Aeneas drove fast, with a sense of purpose.

They got to Seahouses and parked the car near the island tour booking office, now shuttered up against the coming winter. They walked along the harbour wall to where a small fishing boat was tied up. Aeneas carried the basket of food. Brigid climbed into the swaying vessel, which was bobbing ominously even in the protection of the harbour. 'It's not as bad a day as some,' said John comfortingly.

It was relatively protected here by the harbour wall, but once they chugged out into the bay they moved across the swell, making for the scattered group of Farne islands. One minute the boat rose high on the breaker, then plunged down into a trough, spray steaming over the sides, and each time Brigid was certain that they'd plunge too far down and pierce the surface of the water and be submerged. Aeneas sat beside her, his face set against the elements, smiling whenever she looked questioningly at him. Eventually she caught some of his calm, and anyway the swell subsided as they got away from the shore. It was bitingly cold, but the sun was vaporous and the spray danced with ethereal rainbows. Aeneas pointed out the shags, great black birds holding their wings out from their sides, as if to dry.

'I'll show you the seals,' said John, who was a man limited of conversation outside his work. 'Them's breeding.' He pointed out the pups, which were smaller, but still sturdy. Fragile baby mammals couldn't survive these seas. The adults swam alongside and reared up inquisitively in the water, gazing out with their dog-like eyes, full of intelligence and innocence. In the water they were graceful. On land they were clumsy and out of control as they flopped off the rocks into the sea.

'Seals come where there are Celtic people,' said Aeneas. 'Where their songs are understood. Theirs is music of the soul. Hear them singing of the sadness of the world, yet see the joy in their eyes.'

'I had an aunt like that once.' Brigid remembered Aunt Roo and how she'd wished she was more like her. At last, perhaps she was.

The boat landed at St Cuthbert's cove. Brigid hoped to see Cuthbert's cell, but it was long gone, replaced by a cluster of buildings for the wildlife wardens. There was a small museum in a hut for the summer visitors.

The wardens, three young men dressed against the weather, were leaving. They went every four days to monitor the breeding colonies on the outer Farne islands, hoping to limit the breeding grounds and avoid a cull to protect the fish.

'Chris spotted an albino pup,' one of them said to John. 'I doubt it'll survive. It may be abandoned. We don't know.'

'Never seen an albino,' said John. 'I'll go on with you. Coming?'

'Call back for us,' said Aeneas. 'It's this island Brigid wants to see.'

'Don't you want to see the albino?' Brigid asked.

'It's a lot rougher out there,' said Aeneas.

John looked about to contradict him, but closed his mouth.

As the boat moved away over the water, Aeneas turned back to the island. 'We have it to ourselves,' he said.

'There's the lighthouse,' said Brigid.

'It's mechanized. Men come to inspect now and again. They came last week.'

Walking was limited to the path round the small

rocky outcrop. 'In the spring birds nest everywhere, you almost tread on them, cormorants and puffins and terns. Now, in the winter only the shag are left.' Around them the waves broke on the rocks, sending up huge curtains of spray, their spume carrying on the breeze. To the north the rocks were sheer. Water funnelled up the crannies, powered by the force of the sea, and cascaded over the seagrass.

Aeneas pulled a bench across from the shelter of the museum building so that they could look out to the Outer Farne islands. They were dark, remote, wintry already in the sea.

The soup warmed them, and they slurped it noisily in the cold air. They tore off hunks of soda bread and didn't notice the crumbs. 'I think about Si,' said Brigid. 'Where did he go wrong?'

'Same as everyone else. He wanted certainty.'

'He thought he *knew*.'

'The world isn't ready for the New Age. Needs to be better educated. There'll be a lot of messiahs. People glimpse another plane and want to pin it down. If you frame the unknown in terms of this world, it ends up smaller than it should be. It's better to *sense* what might be. Anything is possible.'

'Is that sitting on the fence?'

'Cedric would say it was. Hilly, too. I'm more positive. We live in this world and we don't *know* anything about another. We have a touchstone to ultimate reality in the spirit. I think that's as far as you can go.'

'Be more spiritual. Less religious.'

'Be more grown up, not need to depend on fixed values. Learn to swim without waterwings.'

'Arm bands?'

'Certainly not. Doesn't have the same impact. Waterwings. Learn to swim without their waterwings.'

'People need their waterwings,' said Brigid.

'Only if they don't learn to swim.'

'I may have learned to swim.'

'We're in the world. We should live in it,' said Aeneas, and put his arms round her.

When she left Highmoor House, Perdita left a note saying, 'I love you, and I'll bring Xanthe to see you very soon. Your friend Jennifer rang up and asked how you were. I told her you were with a lover. She's ringing back later. Dessi and I will be at the cottage tonight if that's OK, and tomorrow we're going to Alnwick. He's found a flat.'

In the bedroom of the cottage Dessi and Perdita looked down at the sleeping Xanthe, and nothing more existed in the world for them than her snuffling snore and the movement of her fingers as she reached out to touch the world.

'I really like you,' said Perdita, turning away from the baby at last.

Dessi closed his eyes and put his head on her shoulder. 'I'll be good for you. For you both.'

Aeneas said, 'It'll be an hour before John comes back. They won't find the albino pup easily.'

He led her by the hand across the island. There was a flat area below the path where the rock was covered by cushions of the grey leaves of sea campion. Here and there a small white flower still struggled, fragile with its five double petals and green stamens, and as pure as May blossom. Other flowers were replaced by the cobwebby husks of seed purses waving like sepia fairy balloons. Further out, the rocks were covered with ochre lichen, and beyond them the spray spumed up high, dancing to the drumming of the sea. Aeneas led her to the cushioned rocks and they sat down, looking back at the coast towards the north. Lindisfarne was too far away to be visible. Overhead the sky was full of grey clouds, and the wind off the sea was so cold it hurt her face.

'A year and a day,' said Aeneas, 'since I first saw you.'

'When you stared into my car?'

'You noticed me as well?'

'Only because you looked so startled.'

'I was taken aback. You looked out of place.'

'We were both wrong.'

'A year and a day. The test of a Celtic wedding. A man would take a woman for a year and a day. If they got on, she'd be his.'

'We haven't been together for even one day,' said Brigid.

'I've wanted you for all of that time,' Aeneas said simply.

'I've wanted you for most of it,' said Brigid.

Aeneas made a pillow for her out of his waxed coat, and they lay down, below the rim of the rocks, sheltered from the wind. They learned the touch of each other, familiar and strange all at the same time, and wondered that they were together at last with so little discussion, and so much understanding.

He pulled one of the few remaining campion flowers to lie across her hair. 'You even have a bridal wreath,' he said. The fruit and the flowers. The cake and the bouquet. He held up the husk. 'Here are next year's flowers.'

When Brigid came to Highmoor House, she'd been an island, isolated and without joy. She was an island again with Aeneas, but this time complete, not dislocated from the world.

The rock was hard against her back, and no ceiling more beautiful than the grey clouds bounding across the milk-white sky. Brigid knew within her the distillation of joy. Its essence, like a surfer's wave, poised, breathless, delaying, waiting at the brink, then breaking like a crest of spume on the shore, like the foam bursting up the crannies of rocks beyond them. A single spirit merged with the earth, alive in this moment, here, now and as if for ever.

THE END